VEGAS BABY

A STEAMY PROTECTOR ROMANCE

HOT VEGAS NIGHTS

MELANIE A. SMITH

WICKED DREAMS PUBLISHING

Published by Wicked Dreams Publishing
Boise, ID
info@wickeddreamspublishing.com

Kindle eBook ISBN: 978-1-952121-43-2
Paperback ISBN: 978-1-952121-46-3
Hardback ISBN: 978-1-952121-47-0

CONTENTS

1

KIRA

I met Andrei when I was sixteen. Ekaterina sent me to him the first month I couldn't pay for my aerial silks training. She said he'd have work for me I could do in trade. Even at sixteen, I knew what that meant.

So when I approached the club in the seediest part of Tolyatti — which is saying something — I had no illusions about what might be expected of me. I was prepared for anything: waitressing, being fondled by dirty old men who smelled like alcohol and smoke, scrubbing dishes until my hands bled, or … well, worse.

I'd lived with "worse" for years, after all. My father left when I was eight, after my mother was crippled in an accident at the AvtoVAZ factory she'd labored at for years, stating matter-of-factly he didn't need a wife who couldn't even give him sons before she became a lifelong burden.

Needless to say, it was devastating for both my mother and me.

After he left, we moved more times than I could count, relying on the charity of others for shelter and my mother's meager disability benefits and pay from what little work she could manage for food.

With nothing left for the art I'd studied since I was four, I'd taken work under the table at any warehouse, restaurant, or establishment that would pay a scrawny little girl a pittance. Which I used both for my training and to supplement our scant food rations.

It helped us make ends meet … but only until the day my mother gave up. She said the pain was too great to keep going; she had nothing left to give. After a life filled with struggle, rejection, and pain, it was clear her spirit was just as broken as her body.

I was torn, my love and concern for her warring with the misery I endured daily, as well from living a wretched life of backbreaking work that left little time for my art, even when I could afford it. And despite the pain, for my part I couldn't — *wouldn't* — give up. But I said nothing, either because I couldn't bring myself to argue with her in her condition or because I knew it would do no good.

From then on, she used her monthly stipend not on the small amount of food it used to go toward, but for drowning her sorrows in vodka. The paltry amount I was able to make couldn't even keep us fed, much less pay for luxuries like training, or the supplies it required.

So not long after, with fear and courage battling inside of me, I found myself standing in front of Rhapsody. And I walked in to meet my fate.

Andrei Volkov. Thirteen years my senior, with golden brown hair and a smile that won over the hardest of hearts, he was nonetheless every inch the wolf his last name means, and he managed Rhapsody like a vicious patriarch.

Taught by his father, who owned and ruled the club with an iron fist, he proved himself a young yet shrewd businessman. Andrei knew how to serve cheap booze disguised by fancy names and devious recipes to men with too much money and too little sense. He was a loving caretaker of the girls who danced there, even more so of the ones he'd sell to patrons for the night or take home for his own pleasure. And he brutally dealt with anyone who crossed him or attempted to harm what he considered his.

It was a single bout of his vile temper eight years after I started working for him, and three years after my mother died, which forced him to flee Russia forever. Having become his favorite pet, he demanded I go with him. With my mother gone and Andrei my only source of support, I let him take me. To the United States. To the city of sin. To Las Vegas, Nevada. A desert oasis of indulgence, excess, and — most importantly — opportunity.

Now, two years later, my skills as an aerial silk artist pay our bills, though it was Andrei's contacts who got me here. He acted as my manager and used his connections to sign me to *Obscurité*, a dark, circus-like spectacle of costumes, music, and acrobatics of all manner, spinning the senses into a shadowy mix of lust and excitement. Performing in such an eccentric show in a wildly famous location is a dream I never thought to imagine. It's intoxicating. Challenging. Exhilarating. A life lived on the edge, in every sense.

But I want out. Well, out of whatever relationship I have left with Andrei, anyway — the most dangerous part of my existence here. My position with *Obscurité*, however, I long to keep; it's the calculated kind of danger I've lived for since I was a child.

And while Andrei and I were romantically involved for a time, that ended when I grew up. Not in age, but in the realization, finally, at twenty-six, I've been used and abused by him for too long. And it's time to take my power back. Or take it for the first time, perhaps, in my short but difficult life.

Unfortunately, Andrei owns me in ways that are hard to shake. And he likes to remind me of it as often as he can. Like the voicemail from him this morning after I'd left our apartment. The one saying he knows Michael and I are more than partners, despite my (truthful) protests. Even though we're no longer a couple, he still expects to enjoy the exclusive, shall we say, physical benefits of controlling me, though even those episodes are few and far between since

I've wised up. Because, not for the first time, his hate-filled vitriol laced with dark promises almost sent me running.

But in a country where I know precious few people who would help me, where I have a job that is the only part of my life I love, I pushed it from my mind to deal with tomorrow. Or maybe never, if he calms down and sees sense, as he sometimes does.

So instead of focusing on Andrei's latest rage, here I sit, twined in silks, just below the hot lights of *Obscurité's* theater in a glamorous Las Vegas casino. Unlike anywhere else I've lived or worked, it's somehow the only place where I feel like me.

Completely in character, I lazily shift my glance to Michael. He looks back, his bare face still holding the expression it will when we're in full makeup later, waiting for the cue in the swelling, haunting music around us.

I allow the feelings the music, the moment, is meant to invoke to overwhelm my fears and concerns. And knowing what comes next helps too. Because drops are what I live for. The adrenaline. The feeling of freedom. The sense of barely contained control. My entire body fills with delicious tension as it anticipates that note. And when it hits, we fall.

It's a simple but long bullet drop that is both dramatic and thrilling. As I slide through the silks, my inverted gaze snags on a figure in the wings. Andrei, with murder in his eyes.

It distracts my mind enough that years of muscle

memory are overridden. And I don't stop like I should. Instead, as I fear for what he came here to do, my body begins to tumble haplessly as the silks unwind, limbs snagging and pitching in a frenzy of uncoordinated motion.

Time seems to slow as the fabric evades my rosin-coated hands, his fury rendering me into the helpless sixteen-year-old girl it always throws me back to, making it impossible for my mind and body to remember their training. And I keep falling.

2

SEBASTIAN

"SHMC1, we've got a 17-D-3 at 3400 South Las Vegas Boulevard, over."

With a sigh, I depress the button on the com. "Roger that, dispatch. We'll be there in five, over."

I tap on the window behind me. "Ty, we're up." I check my dashboard and flick on the lights as I hear the rear doors close, followed by the passenger door opening and Ty sliding into the cab.

"What've we got?" he asks, sounding as tired as I feel at the end of a long workday.

"A 17-D-3 at The Mirage." I pull smoothly out of The Tower Resort and Casino driveway where we'd just finished tending to an old lady who fainted with shock when she'd won seventeen million dollars on a Megabucks slot machine. I chuckle as I remember how she woke up and immediately started whooping and dancing around. Obviously, she'll be fine.

Now back on the Strip, even with the lights and sirens blaring, unsurprisingly barely anyone pulls over.

"Twenty minutes left on shift, and we couldn't catch a break," Ty grumbles as I nudge up behind a seemingly clueless pickup truck.

I shoot him a smirk for voicing my exact thought. But then, this is how it goes almost every shift, so I'm not sure why either of us are surprised.

"That's Vegas, baby," I joke.

He rolls his eyes in response, and I chuckle as I focus on navigating us the short distance to our destination.

As per usual, I pull up to the valet entrance of the hotel and a porter is waiting. Ty hops out while I shut down, grabbing the trauma board and scoop stretcher. As soon as I join him, he tosses me the jump bag. Without a word, the porter jogs in and we follow, through the atrium and across the casino floor to the theater.

As we enter, I can see people on stage, talking in urgent voices around a fabric-covered heap on the floor. A woman and two men are crouched around the prone figure.

"We got a call for an unconscious fall victim," Ty says, setting his board down.

The woman and one of the men, both in black leotards, nod bleakly. The other man rises and takes a step back, looking grim.

"We were practicing for tonight's show," the man in the leotard offers, running a hand agitatedly through his short, blond hair. "We've done this hundreds of times. I don't know what went wrong."

I kneel, letting the bag rest on the floor beside me.

"What's your name?" I ask the male performer.

He swallows hard. "Michael. Michael Long."

"Don't worry, we're going to take good care of her, Michael. How long has she been unconscious?" I ask, pulling gently at the layers of silk over her, obscuring all but slivers of her here and there.

"Maybe eight or ten minutes?" the woman offers, shaking her head. "I don't know exactly."

"Did anyone move her?" Ty pipes up, pulling out his scissors when he realizes the fabric is wrapped around her and will need to be cut away for us to assess her condition.

"No," Michael responds. "Jeanie only pulled the ribbons off her mouth to make sure she was breathing."

I grimace as the shears rip through the iridescent fabric. "How far did she fall?"

"I mean, the controlled fall is only about fifteen feet," the woman — Jeanie, presumably — responds. "But she didn't stop like she was supposed to at the end and was still ten feet off the ground. But she —" she chokes on her words a bit "— she landed almost directly on her head."

Michael grimaces. My eyes flick up to the guy behind him.

"I'm the stage manager," he explains, handing Ty a business card. I try not to roll my eyes. "I had everyone else leave the theater to avoid a scene."

I refrain from responding, not because his tone makes me want to call him out for caring more about legalities and appearances than one of his performers, but because Ty is done cutting her out of the silks.

"Still unconscious," Ty confirms.

I grab a cervical collar and immobilizer from the bag as Ty prepares the scoop stretcher.

I look at her fully then, noting her dark hair half out of its binding and strewn around her, her lips parted. A slight crease appears between her brows, and I get a feeling I can't explain, like something in the room shifts, except nobody has moved.

"I think she may be coming to," I tell Ty.

He gives me a questioning look but doesn't get to say anything before a small, feminine groan slips out of our patient's mouth and her dark lashes flutter on her full, high cheeks.

Ty raises an eyebrow. "Well, how about that."

I huff out a breath and look up at Michael. "What's her name?" I ask him.

"Kira," he replies in a quiet tone laced with fear.

I nod and look back down. "Kira? Can you hear me?"

Her thick lashes part and her body shudders with

movement as she bunches up to rise. Ty and I each hold her arms gently down.

"Don't move," I instruct her firmly.

"I fell," she says in a hoarse, barely audible whisper. Her eyes open and her gaze meets mine.

Whatever response I was about to give dies on my lips. We stare at each other, probably only for a moment, but it feels like more. Like recognition. But I know I've never seen her before. I'd remember such a stunning face and such deep, dark eyes filled with the kind of confusion and pain that takes a lifetime to settle in so profoundly.

"You remember falling?" Ty asks.

His voice snaps me out of my trance.

Kira blinks rapidly. "Yes … I …" She trails off, lifting her head to look toward the theater as if searching for something, but winces in pain.

With a deft motion I cup the back of her head in one hand and slide the cervical collar under her with the other.

"This will keep you still until we get to the hospital." I clip it in and reinforce it with the immobilizer.

Ty comes around to place the other half of the scoop stretcher on my side. "Does anything else hurt?" he asks.

Kira's tongue darts out to moisten her lips. "N-No," she stutters. She flexes her fingers and her legs shift. "At least, I don't think so."

The more she speaks, the more her Russian accent becomes clear. It reminds me suddenly of a patient we had who hit his head and woke up with a German accent he didn't have before. Though hers is probably real. Either way, I keep the thought to myself, waiting for Ty to do his thing.

Finally back on his side, Ty slides his half of the stretcher under her as I do mine.

"I'm going to roll you," I tell her. "Let us know if anything hurts." I gently hold her arm and lift and turn her only just enough for Ty to get his part of the stretcher under her, then do the same with mine. I shift to hold her head while he clips the halves back together, then we put her onto the trauma board and strap her down. She doesn't make a sound. I breathe a sigh of relief. If she can remember, and nothing else is broken, those are good signs.

"Okay, Cliff Reed," Ty says acidly to the stage manager. "We're taking her to Sunrise Hospital. Is someone coming with her in the ambulance?"

Michael looks like he's about to ask to come, but the stage manager shoots him a look. "No, we have to see to tonight's show," he replies sharply.

The woman, Jeanie, shoots Michael a sympathetic look. "I'll go find her bag in the dressing room and get it to her in the hospital," she promises.

"And I'll let Andrei know," Michael offer in Kira's direction.

Kira's eyes go terrifyingly wide. "No," she rasps. "I mean … I'll let him know. Once I'm there. That … I'm okay."

Ty shoots me a look. But I didn't need it to recognize the fear in her voice.

"We'll make sure she has a chance to notify whoever she needs," I promise, signaling to Ty. Together we lift her. And then we get her the hell out of there as fast as possible.

I'm silent as we load her up and start back into Strip traffic, lights and sirens on and still doing too little to get us away. Get her away.

Something about the whole situation is just … wrong. I make a mental note to tip off her nurse about this Andrei dude, though I know the nurses ask all the "do you feel safe at work/home" type questions anyway. But just from Kira's reaction, I'm not sure she'd answer them truthfully.

"Well, I know what you're doing after shift's up," Ty murmurs through the open partition between us.

I huff out a noise of agreement. Even with the surliest patients, I'm concerned and attentive. But something in this woman's eyes, in her attempt to keep others from involving this Andrei character, and just my general feeling about the situation has my protective instincts roaring. And I'm not going anywhere until I know she's going to be safe.

3

KIRA

While I wait for test results that could doom my career and my life, I find myself more concerned about what Andrei will do when he finds out he didn't manage to kill me. Will he be horrified and regretful? Or angry that I'll no longer be able to serve his needs when *Obscurité* severs my contract?

I fight back tears of anger and regret. How did I let my life come to this? How did I end up so completely at his mercy, to the point where he could make me lose focus? And not just in that moment on stage. I've lost focus in my life. Of myself.

A fact that presented itself with startling clarity when I came to. When I opened my eyes and found the kindest, most sincere ones staring back at me. Eyes that held true compassion, concern and … something else. They held emotions I've longed to feel.

It was a stark demonstration of the fact that I can't remember anyone looking at me like he did in a very long time. Possibly not since I was a child, cared for and protected by my mother. And it was also a wake-up call to how dead inside I've become. Except for the fear.

My moments on stage have sustained me. But it's been an ephemeral passion flitting along the surface of the deep lake of anxiety inside me. A feeling so vast and penetrating that real, positive emotions couldn't sink in far enough to make a difference, not really.

The doctor coming to talk to me forces me out of my self-pity long enough to hear I have something he calls a "grade III neck sprain." Apparently, this is supposed to be a good thing, since it means I didn't break my neck, my spine, or sustain any brain damage.

They'll keep me overnight for observation, then I'm to rest, ice, and take medication to reduce swelling for three days. I also need someone there at all times for those three days to make sure I don't injure myself further. Followed by eight *weeks* of physical therapy before the doctor will do tests to decide if I'm healed enough to return to the show.

I should be glad I'm alive and my injury wasn't as bad as it could've been. But as I quietly cry myself to sleep, in pain and still wondering how I'm going to face Andrei, Cliff, and everyone else, I can't help but wish the fall had killed me.

When I open my eyes to the bright light of day streaming through the plastic blinds of my hospital room, it takes me but a moment to realize there's a man sitting in the chair below them, a fuzzy silhouette to my just-opened eyes.

Panic tightens my chest, and I make to scramble upright when the gentle tug of the cord winding into my arm and a sharp bolt of pain radiates from my neck up the back of my head and down the length of my spine, freezing me in place. *I'm trapped.* The thought sends waves of terror through me.

Despite the necessary stilling of my body, the panic burrows deeper, feeling like steel bands around my chest, causing my thoughts to race, my breathing to come in short, sharp gasps.

"Hey," the man says, rising. "You're okay. You're safe."

The voice is unfamiliar. Soothing. Not Andrei. My body sags with relief and tears prick the backs of my eyes.

I blink hard, clearing the haze of my panic. I look up. And it's those same eyes I woke to on stage. Dark and warm and full of feeling. My eyes take in the rest of him. Short, dark hair. Thick, arched brows over those hypnotic eyes. Angular cheekbones. A sharp nose and jaw. He looks no more than a few years older than me.

I swallow thickly, my memories of yesterday coming back. He rescued me. A … medic?

"I'm Sebastian Hernandez," he offers. "I was one of the paramedics who brought you in yesterday."

My brows pull together, confused. Had I asked my question out loud? I didn't think I had. And yet, he answered it.

He smiles gently, hovering between the chair he'd occupied and the bed as if approaching an unfamiliar animal he doesn't want to bite him.

"Thank you," I manage. My voice scrapes out of my throat in a hoarse mockery of my usual tone, and it makes me cringe.

"Would you like some water?" he offers.

I almost nod before remembering the pain. "Yes, please."

He reaches behind the bank of monitoring equipment next to my bed and emerges with a full glass of water and straw. Embarrassingly, he lifts it to my lips and helps me drink. And drink I do, draining the glass quickly.

The cool liquid feels like life. My head clears slightly, and my throat relaxes.

"Thank you," I repeat.

"Part of the job," he replies. After he sets the glass down, he pulls the chair he'd been sitting in closer to the bed and settles back onto it.

I raise a suspicious eyebrow. "And do you always visit the people you help in their hospital rooms?"

He huffs a laugh out of his nose and smiles. It's sunshine and hope, and my concern lessens at the sight.

"Not always," he admits. "Just when I feel like they might still need my help."

Now both of my eyebrows rise. "And what makes you think I still need your help?" As soon as the words are out of my mouth, I feel like an asshole. He's just trying to be nice, after all. But he seems to take it in stride.

"Your nurse says you declined to call anyone and didn't list any emergency contacts when they helped you with the paperwork last night," he replies. "And when your friend Michael came to check on you this morning, he said there was only one person he knew to call."

My heartbeat picks up again, knowing exactly who he means. But as skilled as I usually am at hiding my emotions, this stranger clearly knows I'm terrified.

"Don't worry," he says gently, "he didn't call anyone, and neither did we. I told you: You're safe here."

His tone, his expression both tell me he knows how scared I am. How unsafe I am with the only person anyone knows to contact where I'm concerned.

But I don't say anything. I simply nod. Sebastian tilts his head.

"You'll be discharged any time now, and you're going to need someone to take care of you for the next few days. Do you have someone you trust?" he asks gently.

I take a deep breath. "No," I admit. "Can't I just stay here?"

"Not in this room, no," he hedges. "Though there are

facilities associated with this hospital you could go to. But they're usually for post-surgical or elderly patients, and if it's not medically required, insurance won't cover it. And they're expensive."

I press my lips together tightly. Well, that's a no-go since Andrei tightly controls my money. But then, we also still live together, so he'll notice if I don't come home for three days. Hell, he's probably already looking for me now.

"There are other programs," Sebastian says slowly. "For women looking to get out of a situation with a … volatile partner."

My eyes lift to meet his. If only he knew I've been to one of those places already. And when Andrei found me …

"Unless they have something like a witness protection program without the actual witness part, I'm afraid there's nothing you can do," I reply bluntly.

Now it's Sebastian's eyebrows that jump. I realize I may have revealed more than I intended, and I can already tell Sebastian is *very* good at reading between the lines. My eyes drift to the door. As if expecting Andrei to materialize there and take me away to punish me for my words. For not dying. For whatever it is he feels like punishing me for this time.

"Kira."

I ignore his call for my attention, fighting the wave of dread swelling in my chest.

The chair scrapes. I hear him walk to the bed and settle down on it. And his mere presence forces my gaze to his, like I have no control over the decision. His eyes are soft, his jaw set in a hard, tight line.

"You can stay with me," he says. His offer is so shocking I can't keep the surprise off my face. "I know you don't know me at all. But I have a feeling I'm the best option you've got right now. I'm more than qualified to take care of you, and I don't have to work for the next two days."

"That's insane," I reply. Still knowing he's right. Michael is the only person in the show I'm close with — and only by necessity, otherwise Andrei would never allow it —and it'd practically be a death sentence for him to care for me. Andrei would probably kill us *both* if I stayed with Michael. But then, wouldn't he do the same to Sebastian? I shake my head resolutely. I'd rather go back to Andrei, risk his wrath, than put someone else in danger. Especially someone as caring and selfless as Sebastian seems to be. "I appreciate the offer, but I have a home to go to. I will call my … roommate to take me home."

Sebastian's eyes darken. "Can you honestly tell me you'll be safe there?" he asks bluntly.

I blanch at the direct question. "If I stay with you, neither of us will be safe," I respond just as candidly. And I realize I'm not hesitant because I don't trust him. I almost laugh at the absurdity of trusting a virtual stranger more than the man I've known for ten years.

Sebastian leans back, hopefully the truth sobering him to

what his crazy offer would really mean. He's silent for a moment as he weighs my words.

"Now I *definitely* think you need to stay with me," he finally replies.

And to say I'm surprised would be an understatement. Does this guy have a death wish?

"Seriously?" I ask incredulously.

"Absolutely. If it's so dangerous, there's no way I can let you go home."

"*Let* me?" I ask. I sigh wearily, already exhausted from just this small amount of conversation. But then, I've been too tired to fight for a long time. And I may not have the strength to argue with this man. Even though I know he's right. I shouldn't go back there. I should've gotten out long ago.

I have to stop and wonder: Is it cowardice to let someone else try to do what I haven't been able to all this time? To help me get out of Andrei's reach? To take care of myself first?

It's only when I feel a large, warm hand over mine I realize I'd closed my eyes. And possibly drifted off to sleep. In the middle of a conversation.

"Please," Sebastian pleads, his deep voice warm and winning.

I open my eyes and stare back at him. I drag a slow breath in and sigh it out. "Are you really sure?"

"I'm really sure."

The corner of his lips pulls up and it softens me. Even though I don't deserve to be taken care of by someone when all he gets in return is the risk of harm. Unless he's expecting something else.

And even though I don't get any sketchy vibes off him, the thought sends me back to fully alert and awake. "I'm sorry, something just doesn't make sense. What are you getting out of helping me?"

Sebastian pulls his hand back. "I know, it doesn't make sense, does it?" he agrees pensively. "I get from your perspective, my offering to help you is weird. Hell, it's a little weird to me too. And you're in an extremely vulnerable situation. I just want to help, Kira, I promise. I have a one-bedroom apartment. You can have the bedroom. The door locks. If you want I can … I don't know … I can ask the nurses if they can document whose care you were discharged to with my name and address and stuff. Though I'm not sure they'd be happy about me taking a patient home, I don't think it's against the rules or anything."

As I stare at him, trying to figure out the lesser of evils in this scenario, exhaustion creeps back in. And I realize no matter what he says or does, I'm really going to have to trust my gut. Something I used to be able to rely on.

Maybe I still can. Sebastian doesn't feel dangerous. Quite the opposite. He radiates concern and warmth and compassion. I don't think he's offering his help out of anything but the goodness of his heart. It's only because of my own warped mistrust and history I expect him to offer his assistance for the wrong reasons.

Andrei aside, Sebastian is not the kind of man I would associate with, simply because I just don't think I'm worthy of the attention of someone who seems so pure of heart. Because mine was poisoned and warped long ago. It's why I have trouble getting close to anyone anymore … well, when I'm allowed to.

Unfortunately, I know if I go back, I may not survive. Would I have picked these circumstances to make my escape? Not in a million years. But on some level, I know it may be now or never.

"Okay," I say simply.

Sebastian's head snaps up. "Okay?"

"Okay," I repeat, ever so slightly lifting one shoulder.

He nods slowly, not breaking eye contact. "I'll let your nurse know then," he says slowly.

I reach out and find his hand again, this time with mine covering his. I try to contain all the emotions I'm feeling as I say simply, in a shaky voice, "Thank you."

4

SEBASTIAN

"So, this is my apartment."

I step back to let Kira in. I'd have rather helped her walk, but she's stubbornly independent. If I didn't live on the ground floor, I might have insisted. I don't know whether I should admire her for it or be worried about her ability to admit to her limits right now.

The tiny brunette slips inside, and I close the door slowly so as not to spook her. Ever since I saw the fear and mistrust in her eyes during our discussion at the hospital, I've been watching her body language like a hawk. I can practically taste her unease in the tense air around her. It's obvious how badly she wants to run. I don't take it personally.

Her eyes roam over the sparse, utilitarian furniture. Bachelor standard, really, but not bad to look at.

"It's clean," is all she says.

I shrug. "I'm not here much. Basically, just to sleep. Speaking of which —" I point to the short hallway to her right "—the door at the end is the bathroom. The one on the left is the bedroom. You can have a seat wherever you'd like, and I'll change the sheets for you."

She starts to shake her head but hisses in pain. "I don't care," she mutters instead. "I just want to rest."

"You're the boss," I reply, heading down the hall and opening the bedroom door. Sighing in relief when I see I'd remembered to make the bed and there are no dirty clothes on the floor. I open the closet and pull a shirt and a pair of sweats out of a box in the back and hand them to her. She eyes me suspiciously. "I assume you don't want to wear that leotard the whole time. They're clean. You're welcome to wear them. Hell, you can have them for all I care."

She examines the obviously women's clothing in her hands. "I take it whoever these belonged to is no longer around?"

I don't know her well enough yet to know whether she's fishing for information about my relationship status, but in any case, I have no problem giving it to her. It's not like I'm trying to get her in bed. Well, not for sex anyway.

"No, though I honestly don't remember whose they were. There's a whole box of castoffs —" I drag the box out and gesture "— help yourself."

"So you're a man-whore then. Lots of women you don't remember."

Funnily enough, her tone isn't disgusted *or* accusatory. More like amused.

"I wouldn't go that far. But for whatever reason, women have a habit of leaving their clothes here." I shrug, not wanting to be psychoanalyzed over why I keep them. They're not trophies or anything. I just feel weird about getting rid of them. Besides, they obviously came in handy.

"You really don't know why?" she asks, a smile tugging at her lips.

"I guess I never really thought about it. Do you know why?" I say, turning it back on her, somewhat bewildered by the odd turn in the conversation.

"I can guess." I gesture for her to continue, and she smirks. "They're hoping you'll call them and tell them they left their things here, so they have an excuse to see you again. You still have the clothing, which means you didn't call." She pauses, not having told me anything I hadn't already guessed, despite playing dumb. "It also means you probably didn't lead those women to believe they'd get a call."

Now I'm shocked. Not because it's true — which it is — but because she didn't jump to the worst possible conclusion about me. And I'm relieved she might trust I'm a good guy, and she might not be here just because I'm her only option right now.

"You're right. I try to treat everyone with respect and honesty. Even hookups." I consider her for a moment. "You know, if there's anything you want to know about me, just ask. Whatever will make you feel comfortable here."

Kira's eyes drift to the door, as sure as her mind is drifting to fleeing. "I'm not comfortable anywhere," she murmurs, then flicks her eyes to the bed. "But thank you. I think I'd like to sleep now." She climbs onto the bed and sinks into the pillow, cervical collar, leotard, and all, eyes closing wearily.

I watch her for a moment. Just a moment, as I'm struck by how quickly she went from fiercely independent and teasing to this tired, vulnerable woman engulfed by the light-grey down comforter of the bed. Like a dark angel in a hazy cloud, surrendering to the oblivion of unconsciousness. I back out and quietly close the door. I lay my hand on the wood and, for the first time in years, I say the Hail Mary prayer. For her.

Though I haven't gone to church in over a decade, being a born and raised Catholic isn't something that ever completely goes away. So sometimes, just sometimes, when a situation seems particularly dark or desperate, I feel the urge to pray. If anyone could use divine intervention, it's Kira.

5

KIRA

When I wake, I'm momentarily disoriented, not knowing when or where I am. While there's no way to tell the time in the shuttered, dark room, the memories of the last day rush back hard and fast.

My fingers trace the brace around my neck. I can feel the aching, tender flesh beneath it. And for the first time, I'm glad for the reminder I'm alive, and my injuries could've been much worse.

I scooch up on the bed and feel for the lamp I remember seeing on the bedside table. Dim light chases the shadows away as it reveals the basic room. My eyes fall on the clothing Sebastian handed me. They look more comfortable than what I'm wearing. Only true exhaustion would allow me to sleep in the confines of my rehearsal leotard.

I peel it off and replace it with the proffered clothing.

Slowly. Very slowly, as every tilt of my head or shoulders sends bolts of pain through me. But the clothes are soft and smell like spring, instantly soothing me. I stand up carefully, not wanting a repeat of the dizzy spells I had when we left the hospital. Thankfully, the only feeling I have as I rise is hunger. And the need to pee.

I open the bedroom door as quietly as I can, thankful for the bright light washing in from the main area so I can easily see to slip just as quietly into the bathroom. I have to move even more slowly, and performing this most basic of functions is almost too much. But I manage without calling for help. Pathetic though it may be, I feel like it's a small victory toward regaining my independence.

When I emerge, I creep quietly down the short hall and am hit by a wall of aroma that makes my mouth water and my stomach rumble. It's almost too much for my senses, and I all but collapse into the closest chair at the nearby dining table.

I hear footsteps but don't tempt the pain of turning my head, instead waiting for him to come into view. Sebastian sets a plate in front of me, then a glass of water, then a napkin and fork before settling across from me.

"I hope you like Chinese. It's half barbecue pork fried rice, half vegetable moo shu."

I look up at him. He's out of his paramedic uniform and dressed down with a white T-shirt and messy hair. Like he'd been napping on the couch. Here in his own place, he looks more relaxed. More approachable. Though still unobtrusively handsome.

"Thank you," I say quietly. Instead of what I really want to say, which is something along the lines of, *"I don't care if it's dog food, I'm starving."* And then I try not to inhale it like a pig. I sort of succeed, but he seems happy to see me eating either way.

"How long was I out?" I ask after my initial feeding dies down.

He swallows and takes a sip of water. "Well, we got here just before noon. It's almost nine. So, a while."

"You said you don't work for a couple of days?"

"Yes," he confirms.

"So, what would you be doing right now if you weren't saving a damsel in distress?" I ask curiously around the last mouthful of greasy deliciousness.

"I'd probably be having a drink with my partner."

Partner. Of course, he has someone. I don't know why I assumed he didn't just because the clothes didn't belong to his current girlfriend.

"And she's okay with you taking care of some woman like this instead of spending time with her?" I ask, looking down at my empty plate.

"My *work* partner. Ty, the guy who was with me last night when we brought you in."

Relief washes over me. I don't need to add "home-wrecker" to my list of faults. And …

"Was it only last night? It feels like it's been so much longer," I murmur with a sigh.

Sebastian nods slowly. "Time is funny. It seems to move too slowly through the worst times and too quickly through the best."

I huff a dark laugh. "Very true, and it would explain why I feel like I should be eighty-six, not twenty-six."

"I feel that way sometimes too," he replies.

My eyes snap up to meet his. "Why?" I ask, curious. He seems so … settled. Calm. Steady. None of the things I am. None of the things I'd associate with hardship.

But then, such is an ocean. Seemingly serene and soothing, even while powerful currents tear through its depths. And likewise, such are people, I remember as I look at him. You never really know what's underneath the face they show you. Usually not until it's too late.

"I'll make you a deal," Sebastian offers, leaning back in his chair and crossing his arms over his chest, making me all too aware of his powerful physique. In another place, with another man, I'd feel threatened. Yet here, with Sebastian, I don't.

"What kind of deal?"

The corner of his mouth tips up. "I'll tell you my story, then you tell me yours. Or as much of it as you feel like sharing, anyway."

I weigh his offer. It seems fair on the surface, but I'm not used to opening up. Even if I want to. And I'm surprised to find I do want to.

"I can … try," I respond.

He studies me for a moment, and I try not to squirm, to show weakness.

"That's fair," he finally agrees, gesturing toward me. "Go ahead. Ask me anything."

6

SEBASTIAN

The night brings a lot of things I haven't experienced in a long time. Possibly ever. Kira is a quiet person, but maybe that's what makes it so easy to talk to her. I don't get the judgmental feeling I get from most people when I talk about my youth. About growing up poor and surrounded by all the wrong kinds of opportunities. About getting arrested multiple times as a teen for stealing, drinking, and worse. All before figuring out it's not what I really wanted and finally, at twenty-nine, feeling like I have my shit together. Well, together enough anyway.

But my story is *nothing* to Kira's. I know she holds back a lot, but what she does give me blows my mind. What she's been through, what she's *survived* is next level horrific. And I've seen a lot working emergency services in Vegas.

The other side of listening to her talk about these things

in her simple, to-the-point way, with an un-fucking-believably sexy accent is exactly that: sexy. I hadn't fooled myself into thinking I wasn't doing this at least in part because I feel attracted to her. But I haven't thought with my dick in a very long time, and it's not why I decided to help her. Unfortunately, the reality is I'm even more beguiled by her with every passing minute.

She's the exact opposite of every stereotype of a woman who is being controlled by the man in her life, even though he's apparently not technically *her* man anymore. She's strong and willful. She's opinionated and stubborn. Plus, she's dryly funny and even though she's extremely cynical, it's with an edge of realism that's strangely refreshing.

Kira Luan. Even her name is intoxicating. Or I may just be stupid tired, since it's four o'clock in the morning and I've been trying to get to sleep after talking to her all night, then seeing her to bed.

Not in a sexual way, of course. She tried to do everything herself tonight, but I saw the pain in her every movement. And I stepped in gently where I could, including standing outside the bathroom door listening for signs of danger, just like I did when she emerged before dinner. Thankfully my apartment is small, so I could get away from the door before she realized what I was doing.

She's strong. Which is good because she's going to have to be. I can tell she's ready — albeit begrudgingly — to break the cycle with this Andrei fucker. And I want to help her, for all the reasons, right and wrong. I'll just keep the wrong ones to myself, keep things simple, keep it about her. I hope.

I'm woken by a series of thuds that have me springing off the couch and running.

"Shit, shit, shit," in a Russian accent comes from the bathroom.

I knock sharply, despite my concern, not wanting to abruptly invade her privacy.

"Kira? Are you okay?" I call.

"I'm … no," she replies, her voice laced with frustration. "Can you please help?" She chokes out the words like it's the hardest question she's ever asked. And my stomach drops, knowing she must be really hurt.

I take a quick breath, switch to paramedic mode, and open the door.

The room is filled with steam from the running shower. The shower curtain and rod lay askew, half in the tub, half out. And Kira is splayed in the end of the tub, completely naked.

I avert my eyes, noting her cervical collar on the counter.

"You weren't supposed to take your cervical collar off. And sponge baths only. Didn't they tell you?"

"They told me," she grumbles.

"I'm going to have to look — and touch — to help you," I warn her. "I promise to only do what I need to though, okay?"

"Yes, please," she says in a pleading voice filled with pain. "It hurts." She whimpers, and her distress almost undoes me.

With her permission and obvious agony, I snap into action. I grab the towel from the rack and lay it over her slick body. I grab another from shelf next to the sink and use it to scoop her into my arms and out of the tub.

"Hold on to me," I instruct her.

Her wet arms encircle my neck, her head resting on my chest. Her small frame trembles in my arms as I carry her back to the bedroom as quickly as I can, laying her down, the first towel still covering everything private. Even though I got a good eyeful of it all I won't soon forget. *Hostia puta.*

I run my hands lightly over her limbs, checking for breaks or contusions and finding none. "What hurts?"

"My hip, where I fell on it. But mostly my neck," she responds.

"Did you take any more pain meds when you got up?"

"No."

"All right. Just lie still. I'll be right back." I step out and head to the kitchen to retrieve the contoured ice pack for her neck, plus another for her hip. I go back in the bedroom and show them to her. "We're going to ice you." I slip the ice pack around her neck. "Which hip?" She points and I place the other ice pack, then pull the half of the comforter she's not lying on over her.

She sighs in relief. "That's better, thank you."

"Of course. I'll get you some food to take your medicine with, okay? All you need to do is rest."

"Yes, sir," she responds breathily. Joking, probably.

But holy shit. I leave abruptly to disguise the semi her response gave me.

As I make her toast and eggs, I talk myself down. I cannot think of her this way when she's in the position she's in.

It takes considerable effort, but I manage to calm junior down before I bring her a tray of food, drink, and drugs. Because *that* is what she needs.

I head back in and set it down, helping her into a sitting position, then putting her cervical collar back in place.

"I guess I should've asked if you knew what you were supposed to do, but just so we're clear, you have to keep this on for a week. One. Week. No more, no less. No showers. Sponge baths only. And I know they made your first physical therapy appointment for next week, because it was on the discharge paperwork. So, until then, you need to focus on resting and not doing anything to further injure yourself. Got it?"

She blinks up at me, wide-eyed, and I'm suddenly afraid I scared her by being too harsh.

"Got it," she finally replies with a strange expression on

her face. "But I'm fine to be on my own after three days?" And even though she asked a question, she starts eating like she doesn't want to hear the answer.

Shit.

I settle carefully on the edge of the bed. "Hey." She reluctantly looks up at me. "I apologize if I came on too strong just now. I'm just trying to help."

"I know," she replies softly.

"Good. And for the record, I hadn't planned on kicking you out after three days. You can stay as long as you like. But I do have to go back to work tomorrow, which is another reason you need to understand what you are and are not supposed to be doing."

"Yes —"

"*Querida dios*, please don't say 'sir,'" I beg her, an unintended groan slipping out.

And she *laughs*. It's the first time I've heard her laugh, and it absolutely kills me in the best way possible.

"Damn, Kira, it's good to hear you laugh." I didn't mean to say it, but when her face softens, the smile still on her lips, I'm not upset I did.

She doesn't respond, she simply goes back to eating her breakfast, the small smile fixed on her face.

7

KIRA

After breakfast, I manage to work up the courage to turn on my phone, in no small part thanks to Sebastian. Both because I haven't laughed in so long I can't even remember, and because … well, he made it obvious I affect him *that* way. I'd started to wonder. He's such a gentleman, and has made no kind of moves at all, so I figured he wasn't interested in me as more than a good deed or an extension of his work.

It felt good to be wrong, though I can't think too hard on why. Because I'm in no place to be thinking about anyone. Anyone except myself and, eventually, Andrei. Then … then maybe there will be room to think about handsome paramedics who make me laugh.

But right now, phone in hand, I have one purpose only,

which does not include Andrei — yet — so I ignore his texts and voicemails, moving quickly to call Cliff before I am tempted to look at them.

"Kira," he greets me in his gruff way. "It's about time you called. What's going on?"

I roll my eyes. Always to the point, no "*How are you*?" or "*Are you okay*?" — just "*What's going on because this is affecting the show*."

"I apologize for not calling sooner. I was only discharged yesterday and spent most of the day sleeping —"

"I don't want excuses; I want to know what the situation is. Now, I've got Coralie standing in for you, but I need to know if you're coming back, because you and I both know she's not a replacement for you on a long-term basis."

If I didn't know better, I'd say it was almost a compliment. But in this case, it is simple fact, really.

"I might be back in eight weeks," I reply. "It will be up to the doctor whether I'm fit by then, but you have my word I will do everything in my power to be able to rejoin the show as soon as possible. If you'll allow it." And then I hold my breath.

"Well, your contract doesn't allow for an absence longer than a week," Cliff grumbles. "But I suppose we could figure something out. I can discuss the particulars with Andrei."

My throat constricts with nerves, but I push deep and

find my voice. "Can I not negotiate the terms myself? Or does your agreement with him not allow such things?"

"I have no agreement with Andrei, Kira. You've always had me talk to him about anything to do with your contract. It's your contract, you can do what you want, I don't give a flying rat's ass. Come see me next week and we'll sort it out."

It's my contract.

It's *my* contract.

Andrei … the lying *mu'dak* never had any right to any of my money. He only said he did. He took it all from me. And I let him. My rage is ice in my veins as I try to focus.

"I will do that. And please, have you spoken to Andrei since … it happened?"

"No," Cliff says, then pauses. "I don't want to overstep, Kira, but I hope this means you're ending your, er, business arrangement with him."

"I am," I reply emphatically, my chest warming from the closest thing Cliff has ever shown to concern for me. "Or I will. I — I will let him know he no longer has my permission to discuss such things with you going forward."

"Good," Cliff says bluntly. "I'll have Lydia text you when she's set my calendar for next week. Rest up, Kira."

"Thank you, Cliff." *For more than you could possibly know,* I think to myself.

When he hangs up, I turn my phone back off. And I sit, staring numbly at the blank screen.

The knowledge Andrei never managed my contract is both maddening and liberating. How could I let him control me so much I gave up even trying? But then, I've always been a survivor. And I knew with Andrei I would survive, so I didn't push for more. Even though I tired of his commanding behavior quickly, it's only been recently that it started to go beyond comments to actual threats again. At least not since we left home. Since he …

A knock on the door interrupts my train of thought. It's only when I go still that I realize my chest heaves and tears stream down my face, my body clearly grieving all I've suppressed.

"What?" I call tonelessly, too tired and over it to hide my state.

The door opens and Sebastian appears, the picture of concern. "I heard crying."

My brows bunch together before I realize the crying must've been me. It makes sense when I look for it, as I can also feel the rawness of my throat. I must have been sobbing as I came to terms with how foolish I've been.

I sniff deeply, quickly regaining control of myself. "I'm fine."

One of Sebastian's thick, dark brows quirks up. "It's okay to not be fine, Kira. You've been through a lot."

White hot anger rises to the surface. "What do you know? One night where I tell you a little of my past, and you think you know what I've been through? You know nothing.

Stop trying to pretend like you have any idea what's going on. Stop trying to save me." I rise, storming past him and into the bathroom, slamming the door behind me.

And I sink to the floor, overcome with hate and anger and despair, silent sobs wracking my body. Every jarring motion sends pain shooting through my neck, but I don't stop. I can't stop. The floodgates have released.

I don't even hear the door open. Don't even know he's there until he sinks down behind me, wrapping his arms around me until I lean against him. He braces my head and shoulders, and the pain lessens. He holds me there without a word as I let go.

When my tears begin to abate, I know it wasn't about him. Not really. I'd been breaking for a long time. The knowledge I was only at Andrei's mercy because I allowed it was the straw that broke the camel's back, as they say. Or broke me, as it were. And in hitting bottom I threw insults at the man who now sits beside me, all the broken pieces of me in his arms without judgment, without agenda.

At first, shame washes over me. But then, I realize — I can let this undo me, or I can accept the gift of his kindness and use it to get stronger. Even if the idea that I need his help leaves me deeply conflicted. With a sniff, I pull my pieces back together and sit up.

Through watery, puffy eyes, I look at him, unsure of whether to say, "*I'm sorry*" or "*Thank you.*"

But before I can say either, he rises, pulling me gently with him.

"Come on," he says, tugging me out of the bathroom. "I know exactly what you need."

8

SEBASTIAN

"Oh my god, I had no idea," Kira says, sinking back into the couch, happy tears leaking out of her eyes. "You're right, that was exactly what I needed."

With a chuckle, I mute the credits and set aside the empty container of Chunky Monkey. "There's also *Legally Blonde 2*," I offer teasingly.

Her eyes light up. "Yes, please!" she says enthusiastically, then hesitates. "I mean, if you want to."

I stare at her for a moment, holding back what I really want to say. Because after seeing her break down this morning, there's nothing I wouldn't do to make her feel better. But such a strong statement freaks *me* out, so I can't imagine how she'd take it. No, better to keep it light. Easy. Until and unless she's ready to talk about it.

"You think I'd have watched the first one if I wasn't

prepared to watch them both?" I tease instead. "I have two older sisters, Kira. I know the healing power of a good chick flick." I wink and reach for the remote, but she stops me with a hand over mine.

"Thank you, Sebastian. And I want to apologize —"

I hold up a hand. "You have nothing to apologize for. You weren't wrong. I don't really know what you've been through."

"Still, I am sorry," she insists. "You've been kind. And obviously I do need your help. I had no right to speak to you in anger. I was just upset."

"I understand," I assure her. I resist telling her I know how she feels because I don't. Though I have hit rock bottom a time or three, so I know what that part feels like. And it has to be you who wants to climb out. Nobody can do it for you. "You're allowed to feel everything you're feeling right now. I'm not going to hold anything you say against you. I know this isn't easy for you. I'm not going anywhere."

Her dark lashes flutter and suddenly, to my surprise, she's crawling into my lap and wrapping herself around me. I can feel the gratitude and relief in her embrace, and I can't help but kiss the silky, dark crown of her head. As much as I've tried to keep a polite distance, I'm relieved. Because it's hard not to feel protective and affectionate toward her. And it feels good to know she feels that way too.

"Sebastian?"

I pull back and look into her eyes. "Yeah?"

"Let's order pizza and watch the movie. Yes?"

I laugh and shake my head. Fucking hell. Under any other circumstances, I would've kissed a girl for saying that. "Sounds like a plan."

So we watch chick flick after chick flick until she falls asleep on the couch, leaning against me. I know she enjoyed the movies, but I also got the sense she wanted to avoid thinking about anything else, much less talking about it. Something else I understand, which is why I didn't question her. Even though I'm curious as fuck what set her off this morning. And what she plans to do about the dark cloud named Andrei hanging over her head. It's good I have to go back to work in the morning because otherwise my curiosity might get the better of me, and I don't want to push her before she's ready.

I pick her up carefully, marveling at how light she is in my arms, how the worry which always tightens her eyebrows and lips is smoothed away in sleep. I gently tuck her into bed, closing the door behind me. And in what I'm pretty sure is going to become a ritual, I touch the door and say another prayer for her.

We fall into a routine for the next three days where I work, spend all day wondering how she's doing, then bring home dinner only to spend the whole night talking with her, watching movies, or whatever she wants to do. I don't know if it's her pain levels and ability to move getting better, or because she's had solid time and distance from her abuser, but every day it seems like she's more alive, more energetic, more talkative.

And the more she opens up about herself — her past, her passion for her work, her desires — the more I want to know. The more questions I have, most of which I never voice because they skate too close to the few subjects she avoids or shuts down completely, all having to do with the future, both immediate and distant. But she asks me plenty of questions of her own, all of which I answer.

Every night she falls asleep leaning against me on the couch. And every night I carry her to bed, then say a prayer for her.

On the third night — well, really, the fifth night since she's been here, the third since I started back at work — as I'm settling her into bed, she stirs.

"I forgot to tell you," she mumbles, eyes opening halfway. "My physical therapy starts tomorrow."

I sit down next to her and nod, smoothing the comforter over her. "I know. I'll be back by three to get you there in time."

She smiles up at me sleepily. "Thank you, Sebastian, you're always so thoughtful." She yawns and rolls onto her side, curling into a ball and falling promptly back to sleep.

I tuck a lock of hair behind her ear, stroking down her long tresses. She sighs in her sleep as my hand slips over her shoulder, and something tugs inside my chest. I try to push it down, but it tugs harder.

I realize I've become more than just protective of her. My need to know what she plans to do next isn't just about my concern for her safety. Despite telling myself I'm only helping her because it's the right thing to do, I can't deny how good I feel around her. Not because she's a charity case who makes me feel benevolent. But because of who she is: a strong, clever, and deeply passionate woman with a gift for blunt honesty that knocks me on my ass. And an internal, delicate beauty that when given room, outshines even her stunning exterior.

Unfortunately, the realization changes nothing. Kira has enough on her plate. It wouldn't be fair to tell her I'm falling for her. Not now.

I lean down and kiss her hair, inhaling the same shampoo scent I use, though it somehow smells better on her. And I leave, saying a prayer at her door before I head back to the couch, where sleep takes a long time to find me.

9

KIRA

I will never get used to waking up to an empty apartment. To being alone all day. To doing nothing. Well, not without my every move being watched, my every choice being questioned. This simple freedom has given me a lot of time to think. It's all I've done while Sebastian is away every day. It's been exactly what I needed.

Because later today I'll leave this sanctuary for the first time since I came here. Ready or not, it's time. And it's also time to deal with everything I've been ignoring.

I breathe deeply, in through my nose and out through my mouth, steadying myself just as I would before a performance. And I turn on my phone. A slew of new messages appears. I read the only one not from Andrei first.

Kira, it's Lydia, Cliff's assistant. He'd like to meet with you Wed 2 pm in his office. Please let me know if you can make it. Thanks, hope you're feeling better.

Heart swelling with gratitude, I immediately reply I'll be there. And then I check to see how far of a walk it is to The Mirage. My heart sinks when my phone tells me it's more than three miles. Normally I wouldn't bat an eye, but even though I *am* feeling better, I'm not stupid; I'm not better enough for that much exertion. Thankfully, a little more investigation shows a bus line along East Flamingo that cuts the walking down to a manageable amount.

Satisfied, I steel myself as I look at the dozens upon dozens of messages from Andrei. I decide to read the texts first.

While they're nothing I didn't expect, my stomach turns to lead as I go through the nearly six-day-long litany of Andrei's descent into madness.

Horror at watching me fall. Meaning he stayed and watched me fall. And his words imply he didn't intend to make me fall. But still he ran, like a coward.

Then pleading to know I was alive and okay. As if he cares.

Then when he got no response, anger and threats.

I'm nothing without him.

He owns me.

I owe him.

He'll find me.

Then regret and apologies.

I'm so sorry.

You're my everything.

Please just tell me you're okay.

And back and forth. On and on. The threats getting worse until they're against my life. Until they're explicit in all the ways he'd like to hurt me.

Likewise, the apologies get more pathetically sorrowful at how he can't help himself; this is what he turns into without me.

I set the phone down without listening to the voice messages. I don't need to hear them. Or maybe I can't stand his wretched ranting anymore.

Because through reading the sad pile of messages, I shed not a single tear. All I felt was pity for how small his world has become that I'm the only bastion of control left in his life. And I also feel fear because I'm not stupid; Andrei is dangerous. But his vitriol doesn't have the same effect on me any longer. I'm not going to be manipulated by him for another moment. The rest I'll worry about later. Because I know this isn't going to end easily, or well. But it will end.

For now, I think about my response. I think so long that the sun moves over the building, and the bright yellow morning light that streamed through the bedroom window dulls into the golden hues of late afternoon.

When I'm ready, I type my message. Firmly, and with strength in my heart, finally.

I am alive. I am healing. But I have learned you never

had any right to my contract, or my money. I am done being controlled by you. I am not coming back. Please do not contact me ever again.

Feeling empowered for the first time possibly ever, I shut off my phone.

Physical therapy is nothing like I expected it to be. Compared to the grueling training regimen I've endured my whole life, moving my head up and down, side to side, and tucking in my chin repeatedly to rebuild the stabilizing muscles of my neck is nothing. Even the dull pain it incites is nothing, not in the grand scheme of things.

"I know this may seem silly," Peter, my physical therapist, says as he watches me do the exercises. "But today is just about baselining your range of motion and pain levels. When you go home, you'll do these every day until our next appointment. And every time we meet, we'll do increasingly difficult exercises."

"For eight weeks?" I reply.

"That's the general guideline, yes. But if you need to go slower, we will," he responds.

"And if I need to go faster?" I ask.

Peter smiles tolerantly. "I know how it's hard to be patient with your body, but it's very important you don't move too fast because it could end up setting you back even further. But if you seem to be progressing more quickly, I'll meet you where you are with the appropriate exercises," he promises.

I dip my chin in agreement, even though it hurts. Just to show I can.

He guides me through another set, correcting my form on the chin tucks so my head is fully over my shoulders, before declaring us done for the day and fitting my neck brace back on. I must make a face because he chuckles.

"One more day," he says. "Wear it through tomorrow, then you're good to take it off. Keep icing. Keep doing your exercises. And I'll see you next week."

I give him a vague smile. "Thank you." I turn to leave, but Peter's hand on my shoulder stops me.

Peter drops his voice and says, "For what it's worth, if you don't overdo it, and you're diligent … I think you could be back to work in six weeks." His hand drops and he gives me a conspiratorial wink.

I beam up at him and thank him one more time before rushing back toward the waiting room to tell Sebastian. Between separating myself from Andrei, finally, and the possibility of getting back to work even sooner, I feel like celebrating. And suddenly I realize the feeling in my tummy isn't just from excitement. It's also the realization that I want to see Sebastian's face light up that has me running to tell him.

10

SEBASTIAN

When Kira walks back into the reception area, she's beaming. My shoulders sag with relief, alerting me to exactly how tense I'd been. I rise to meet her.

"We need to celebrate," she says immediately, her eyes filled with life and hope.

I smile down at her. "Well, therapy must've gone well," I tease.

"It did," she confirms.

"Good. I assume they warned you you'd be a little more tender after, so we can't go too crazy." I say it like I'm hesitant, but I'd already been planning something for the rest of the day even before her request, as when we left the apartment for her appointment, I couldn't help but notice how much being outside affected her. Even though it must've hurt, her head turned this way and that, her eyes wide, a smile on her face while she looked at the world around her as if with new eyes.

And it occurred to me she does have new eyes. She survived a fall that could've permanently disabled or killed her. That kind of brush with death changes you. And her being alive and on the path to recovery is something to celebrate.

She rolls her eyes. "I promise I'll take it easy."

I raise an eyebrow and give her a sly smile. "Good, because I already had something in mind. That is, if you're up for a drive."

Her eyes go wide. "As in, leave Las Vegas?"

"Yes, ma'am."

She bounces on the balls of her feet. "Let's go!"

I can't help laughing. I've never seen her so excited. I gesture for her to precede me out. Let the mini adventure begin.

Thirty minutes later, as we pass through Boulder City, Kira perks up from her silent perusal of the landscape and stares straight ahead.

"Is that … water?" she asks, leaning forward as the blue sparkling mass appears on the horizon.

"Lake Mead," I confirm. "I take it you haven't been here before, then?"

"No," she says quietly, entranced. "I haven't been … anywhere, really."

I frown and make a mental note to rectify that. "It's one of my favorite quick escapes. You'll see."

We keep driving, stopping at the park entrance where I show my pass and ID to get waved through. Kira pays the stop no mind, her eyes fixed on the lake to our right. I smile as I pull forward, glad she's enjoying it.

I watch her out of the corner of my eye for the last few minutes of the drive, her excitement getting more and more palpable as we pull into the dirt parking lot at the marina entrance.

"Are we going on a boat?" she asks, awe and excitement in her tone.

"Not today," I say with a laugh. "But there's a café on the harbor with a great view. You okay to walk a bit?"

She turns a shining smile toward me. "Yes," she replies simply, then hurries out of the car.

The late October afternoon is pleasantly warm as we head toward the harbor walkway. Kira looks a little reticent as we step onto the stone pavers of the relatively narrow path over the water. Both of her arms snake around my right one, gripping tightly.

"It's safe," I assure her, reaching my free hand over to squeeze one of hers.

She smiles nervously up at me but allows me to lead her the few minutes' walk to the café. When we're almost there, we pass a couple of kids sitting on one of the wooden boat platforms jutting off the harbor walkway, tossing popcorn to a writhing mass of fish below.

Kira gasps and without a thought, stops and leans over the edge to watch. "I've never seen fish act so crazy. What are they?"

"Carp," I respond. "They're demanding *pendejos*, since they're used to people feeding them. It's kind of a thing here. Do you want to try it?"

She straightens up, seizing my arm again, as if suddenly realizing how close to the water she was. "Maybe later," she murmurs.

I chuckle and lead her on, into the café.

To my surprise she orders their Titanic burger — the biggest, messiest burger they have. And it's also delicious, so I order one too.

We find a table and sit, waiting for our food as we sip on Cokes.

"So, did the PT say anything else? Any specific concerns?" I prod as she's been silent pretty much since we left.

She shrugs lightly. "I have exercises to do. He told me to be patient and not push too hard, or I won't be able to go back to work for longer."

I raise a brow. "And that's your plan? Going back to the show?"

She leans back into her chair, wrapping her arms around her. "Yes, I hope to. I'm meeting my stage manager tomorrow afternoon to discuss my contract."

Well, color me surprised. "I'm glad to hear it. Do you need help getting there?"

"I can manage, but thank you."

"Of course," I reply.

"I was also thinking I should find another living situation. Maybe one of the … services you suggested?" She looks down at her drink, avoiding eye contact.

I shift in my chair, concerned I've done something to make her want to leave.

"Uh, sure, of course, whatever you want. But I mean, you're welcome to stay with me until you get back on your feet." It's not what I'd originally planned, but suddenly the thought of her leaving is unbearable. My chest tightens with the realization, but I also recognize I'm pushing my own selfish agenda in trying to keep her around. "Though I get you probably want to be out on your own. Whatever you want." And now I'm repeating myself like a moron.

Thankfully, one of the employees drops off our burgers, so I'm spared making a bigger ass of myself while we dig in. And holy hell is it just as good as I remember. A thick, juicy patty with two types of cheese, bacon, onion, chili peppers, and all the trimmings.

"Oh my god," Kira groans after her first bite, juices from the meat dribbling down her chin.

I grin despite my full mouth. She rolls her eyes with delight and takes another huge bite. It doesn't take either of us long to devour the giant burgers *and* the giant piles of fries that came with them. I'm impressed someone so tiny could take down a meal so huge no problem.

As the carb overload sets in, we chat about other, less serious topics. Where else Kira hasn't been in the area she needs to go. Her other favorite foods. What chick flick we should watch tonight. It's nice. And as we walk back along the harbor, with her arms now gently entwined with mine, it feels more like a date than anything else. God, I wish.

"So … are we feeding the fish?" I ask slyly.

She scrunches her nose. "Okay."

I steer her into a shop a bit down the path, and we get a bag of popcorn then head to the spot the kids had occupied earlier. The fish are still thick in the water, clearly waiting for their next meal.

Kira settles in, legs folded under her, before tossing a handful of food to them. She laughs with delight as the carp writhe and flop over each other, battling for the tiny morsels. I settle in beside her, watching her. The joy on her face is captivating.

When she's run out of treats for her new fishy friends, she leans back, looking out over the water.

"I messaged Andrei today. I told him I'm not coming back, and he needs to leave me alone."

I sit up to attention, taken aback by how abruptly and casually she dropped the information. But I have no idea what to say about it.

She turns to me, her dark eyes troubled. "It's why I should leave, Sebastian. He *will* find me. And I cannot bring that to your doorstep. Not after everything you've done for me."

My heart sinks. Before I can stop myself, I lean forward, cupping her face in my palm. "All the more reason you should stay. How can I protect you if you're not with me?" I didn't mean to say it, even if it's what I feel. Because it reveals too much.

She closes her eyes and nuzzles into my palm. "I will manage. He only knows where I work, and I can be … careful where that is concerned. You've done enough. You do not need to take on the burden of protecting me more than you already have."

I stroke my thumb over her cheek, and she opens her eyes. "And if I *want* to?"

Her lips part. Her eyes search mine. "Why?" she whispers. "You barely know me."

I shake my head. "I may have met you only a week ago, but from the moment you opened your eyes, I felt like I knew you. Even though you have so much to deal with right now, and I don't want to scare you off … I care about you. I want to be here for you, in whatever way you'll let me."

A sigh escapes her lips, and then they're on mine. Soft and supple and warm. The taste of her has me wanting to thread my fingers through her hair, pull her to me, and claim her. But I hold back. And when she pulls away, I'm left feeling like her kiss was everything and yet not enough.

"I'm sorry. I shouldn't have. I … I can't …" she trails off, her voice catching, the conflicting emotions obvious in those expressive eyes of hers.

I run a thumb over her bottom lip and then let her go, sitting back. "We don't have to start anything now. Whatever this —" I gesture between us "— is can wait until you're healed and in your own place. I don't want you to feel any pressure from me, so you know you can stay. This can wait. I can wait. But what I can't do is let you face your recovery — and your ex — alone."

Kira's lips droop into a frown that makes me want to kiss it away. God, I want to kiss her again so badly. To show her how much I care for her, want her, need her.

"I don't deserve you," she murmurs. "But I accept your offer. Gratefully."

I take a deep breath and rise, extending my hand to help her up. "Let's go home."

Kira takes my hand and rises. She pauses as if she wants to say something, but nothing comes out. I stare at her, the force of what she does to me hitting me fully, my heart aching with everything I want. For myself, for her, for what happens next. But instead of saying what's on my mind, I lace my fingers in hers and we walk slowly back.

The drive is silent but not uncomfortable. When we get back, there's no talk of watching a movie. There's hardly any talk at all. She simply bids me goodnight and goes into the bedroom. When the light goes out a moment later, I walk to the door, place my hand on it, and silently pray.

11

KIRA

I don't wake on Thursday since I never went to sleep in the first place. Want and guilt warred within me, robbing me of sleep. Because I wanted Sebastian last night, badly. So badly I agreed to stay. How could I not feel guilty for continuing to put him in danger?

I cannot say exactly what I feel for him besides want, though. It's hard to separate my emotions out these days. I have so many, even besides the pain, the fear, and the hope that has only recently begun to illuminate the darkness of my life.

Part of that hope is because I finally have the distance and space I've so desperately needed to see things clearly. But another part of that hope is, undeniably, because of Sebastian. I don't want to be alone as much as he doesn't want me to be. But I don't just want *someone* to not be alone with. I want *him*. Because being alone has never scared me before. I think … I think I don't want to lose him as much as he doesn't want to lose me. I've come to need him, and it scares me. Not for my own heart, but for the peril it puts him in. I hate myself for wanting to be near him, for risking him.

Unfortunately, leaving causes just as many problems as staying. It's a conundrum I'll have to deal with another day. Today, I take back another part of my life: my career.

At the thought, I rise with purpose, cleaning and dressing myself before having a light meal and getting ready to leave. I notice an envelope taped to the door as I go to open it.

I look inside and find a key and a note which simply says "yours." I clutch the small, metal gift in my fist and hold it to my heart.

And then I head out to meet my fate.

The journey is both challenging and invigorating. Such small accomplishments, finding the bus stop, riding the bus, walking to the theater. I have to go slow, as my pain creeps higher the more I exert myself. But it's good to do these most basic of things again. To rely on myself. To be out in the world.

When I approach Cliff's office, his door is open, and I can hear him typing away. It feels like any other day I've had to speak with him. I hover in the doorway until he looks up.

"Kira. Come in. Sit." He eyes my neck brace and gestures to the chair across from him.

I balance delicately on the edge, leaned forward. Before I can say a word, he plops a sheaf of papers in front of me.

"Here's your amended contract. I got you up to twelve weeks from your last performance to return to the show. Your leave will be unpaid, but I have your check here for the last period you worked. You'll need to submit a doctor's note along with the signed contract and we'll be good to go."

I blink rapidly, trying to absorb the onslaught of information.

"That's it?" I ask bluntly.

"That's it. So long as the signed contract and note are in my hands by the end of next week."

I look at the stack of papers in front of me, at the check paper clipped to the top page. My eyes widen at the amount.

"I … is this right?" I gasp.

Cliff frowns. "I know it's not the full check you're used to, but you only worked a little more than half the shows you'd normally be paid for."

My jaw drops and I look up at him. I usually make *twice* this? I lift the stack, clutching it to my chest for a moment before carefully placing it in my bag.

Cliff's brows bunch together. "That fucker really was taking your money, wasn't he?" he growls.

I nod sheepishly.

"Yeah, he tried to pick up this check yesterday too. Told him you'd be coming to pick it up yourself today, and I'd be dealing with you and only you from now on," he informs me smugly.

My very blood slows in my veins as I freeze in place. "You told him I'd be here today?" I stand, backing up from the desk.

"Well … I … he …" Cliff stutters, realizing he's made a mistake.

But he has no idea how big of a mistake.

"I have to go," I say.

"Kira, wait!" he calls.

But I'm already gone. Out the door, running through the hall behind the theater as I pull out my phone to call Sebastian, hoping he's able to answer.

"Kira? What's wrong?"

I breathe a sigh of relief when I hear his voice. "Sebastian, I just met with Cliff. He told Andrei I'd be here today. I'm scared. Is there any way you can pick me up?" The words tumble out so fast they are almost incoherent.

There's silence on the other end, and I'm afraid he didn't hear me.

"Get in the casino where there are lots of people, find an employee, and wait with them. I'll call you when I get there."

The anxiety twisting in my chest lessens. "Thank you." I

hang up and slip my phone back into my purse. I turn down the hall to the casino when an arm wraps around me, followed by the unmistakable cool circle of metal touching to my temple. A gun.

"*Ty byla plokhoy devochkoy*, Kira," Andrei's voice hisses in my ear. *You've been a bad girl.* He doesn't know the half of it.

"Let. Go. Of. Me," I grind out angrily. In English. Sending the message: I'm not the scared little Russian girl he rescued from poverty anymore.

"Hm. Let me think," he says, switching back to English. "No." He drags me back toward the dressing rooms, likely because he knows they will be empty with no show today. But I don't intend to go quietly.

"You're not going to get away with this," I cry. "If you kill me, where will you run? You can't go back to Russia, Andrei."

"Oh, Kira, darling, I'm not going to kill you," he says with a maniacal laugh. "I'm just going to beat you so badly you'll never think of leaving me ever again. Because you know I'll always find you."

"Then you'll *have* to kill me because I'm never staying with you. Never!" I screech the words at him.

"Oh, I think you will. I heard you talking to your new boyfriend. How about I wait for him, tie him up, and make you watch what I do to him?" Andrei hisses in my ear.

Knowing he is capable of doing just as he says, my blood runs cold. But it makes me even more determined to get away from him as quickly as possible. Before he can get anywhere near Sebastian.

"Let —" I thrash violently in his arms "— go —" I stomp my feet, trying to find his "— of —" I throw my head back, finally connecting with him in a sickening crack that sends pain through my skull and neck "— me." With a cry of agony, he loses his grip, releasing me. Metal clatters to the floor. I whirl around to see Andrei holding his bloodied nose.

"You *bitch*," he bellows.

I spare him not another glance, diving for the gun on the floor. His yell cost him time, so even though he dives too, I get my hands on it first.

Unfortunately, he's close. Too close. He pins me to the floor, his face in mine, my hands uselessly holding the gun over my head as he scrambles with long fingers to pry it from my grip. He's so much stronger than me, and with his weight pinning me and stealing my breath, I can't resist. The gun slides out of my hands, tumbling to the ground.

Now his hand goes to my throat before he remembers the brace. I take the opportunity to knee him in the balls. I must miss because he groans but doesn't move, choosing to press his hand over my mouth instead.

"You want some of those?" He slides his other hand between my legs, and I scream behind his hand. "I'll give them to you, you little bitch. I'll fuck you so hard you'll remember who you belong to."

His hand covers my mouth and nose as he pulls down my leggings. I scream and thrash and push, but it's no use. My brain starts to go fuzzy from lack of oxygen. I feel a tug at my panties. It's the last thing I register before I pass out.

12

SEBASTIAN

I've never driven so fast in my life. And that's saying something. Even though we were only a couple of miles away, the few minutes it takes to get to The Mirage feel like hours. I'm calling Kira before I'm even fully out of the ambulance, barely registering the concern on Ty's face at my insane driving. Even though I've told him pretty much everything he needed to know about what's going down.

When she doesn't answer, I almost lose it completely. I turn back to Ty.

"Get me police in the theater now. I'm going in," I command.

He opens his mouth like he's going to remind me we're not supposed to go in first, but he apparently thinks better of it and picks up his walkie talkie.

With a grim nod of approval, I run inside, ignoring the surprised looks of several casino employees as I whip by them. I see no sign of Kira along the way, and when I burst through the theater doors, still nothing. My adrenaline pumping, I try to remember the layouts I've been shown before to remember where the offices are.

From behind the door at the back left of the theater, I hear a man yell. My legs move even before my brain can register, my EMT training so deeply ingrained to move toward danger.

I burst through the doors, and halfway down the hallway I see a man with light brown hair on top of a woman with dark hair, either in the process of or about to rape her. Kira. Something inside me snaps. My vision turns red as I let out a roar, sprinting for the bastard.

I tackle him hard, sending us both flying. I land on top of him and hear his head crack against the cement floor. The sound snaps me back to reality.

"Shit," I curse, climbing off him. He's out cold. But I don't tend to him first. I rush back to Kira. She's also unconscious, her leggings torn off but her underwear still intact. Thank God.

I lean over her, checking for breath as I hold her wrist for a pulse. I almost cry with relief when I find both. I hear a call from the theater.

"In here," I roar.

The doors blow open to reveal Ty with the jump bag. He

tosses it to me, and I catch it on instinct. I set it down and begrudgingly turn back to Andrei. Blood is seeping slowly out from under his head.

When Ty reaches Kira, I tell him, "Breathing and pulse are okay. I think he was smothering her. See if you can wake her and check for signs of neurological damage. When you're done, we're going to need the trauma board for this guy. Unconscious with a rear cranial contusion, blood loss, possible concussion. If he doesn't come to before I've got his head wrapped and stabilized, I need you to help me intubate and get an IV going."

"Roger," Ty responds, checking Kira's pupils. Ty pulls away to get the bottle of ammonia inhalant as I work to stop Andrei's bleeding long enough to clean his wound. But a small groan stops us both in our tracks.

Kira sits up before Ty can stop her. She waves him away. "I'm fine," she says, clearly annoyed.

Ty shoots me a wry look at her sass. "I'll be the judge of that," he says to her.

I check Andrei's bleeding and move to clean and wrap him. By the time I'm done Ty has finished checking out Kira. "She's good. No signs of concussion or neurological damage. LVPD is enroute."

I stabilize Andrei while Ty tries to bring him around. When he fails, he begins intubation while I get the IV going. Once we're both done, Ty heads back to the ambulance for the trauma board and scoop stretcher.

"Is he going to live?" Kira asks, scooting toward us carefully.

I look up at her, locking eyes with her for the first time since she regained consciousness. And I almost lose it I'm so glad she's okay.

"I don't think I can officially say I hope not," I grumble. And Kira *laughs*. It's wry and bitter, and a pained laugh chokes out of my throat in response.

"I'm sorry," she says immediately. "It shouldn't be funny. Not after what he just did." She looks down at herself. Luckily her shirt is long enough to cover her thighs.

"*Almost* did," I correct her. "Almost did." I repeat it like it can change that he did, in fact, assault her. Even if he didn't get to the rape part.

Suddenly I hear the LVPD announce themselves, jogging in with Ty hot on their heels. And so begins the lengthy explanation of what happened. I don't even care if I get fired for going in ahead. As we ride to the hospital, with Kira in the front of the ambulance with me, I'm just so fucking glad I got there in time to save her.

I hold her hand tightly the whole way. Hoping I'll get the chance to always be there when she needs saving.

13

KIRA

I wake up and before I even open my eyes, I remember I am in quite possibly the exact same hospital bed I was in at the exact same time last week. Even though Sebastian's partner cleared me at the scene, the doctors insisted on observing me overnight given my recent injury and the potential for further damage, or brain trauma, or something along those lines. Too tired to remember or care, all I want is to open my eyes and find this all was a dream.

I blink the sleep away and scooch into a sitting position. Only to find Sebastian in the very same chair he'd occupied in likely this very same room at this very same time last week.

"Well, this is déjà vu all over again," I joke dryly. But the look on Sebastian's face leaves no room for humor. "What happened? Is he alive?"

Sebastian sighs and rises to resettle on the edge of my bed. "He's alive. And he's going to be just fine." He pauses, a sad, stern air about him. "Why didn't you tell me what he did?"

My heart skips a beat. And it only takes me a moment to understand. "They know," I say. Sebastian dips his head in agreement. A slew of emotions passes through me. Disgust. Relief. Unease. "What's going to happen to him?"

"I don't know yet. *Why didn't you tell me?*" It's the closest to angry I've ever seen him.

"Would it have mattered?" I ask.

"That he tortured and killed your lover while you watched? That he was capable of something so … so …" Sebastian trails off, clearly unable to put words to how awful what Andrei did was.

"Heinous? Unthinkable? Demented? You don't have to tell me, Sebastian. I know. I was there. Why do you think I was so afraid of him? Why do you think I wanted you nowhere near me? Why do you think I hate myself for needing you? For even *thinking* about falling for you?" I yell the words at him as tears stream down my face. But they don't have the effect I intended. If I had any real intent. But his reaction is nothing like I expected.

His mouth descends on mine roughly. His searing, claiming kiss tears through my rage, my defenses, my very soul until I wrap my arms around his neck, begging for him to keep punishing me with his lips, his tongue. To wipe everything else from my mind.

He pulls back long before I'm ready for him to. "You could've *died*, Kira. He could've killed you any time. And I would have never had a chance to fall for you either."

I look up at him with doubt. How? How could someone like him fall for me? I didn't even know I was falling for him until the words just tumbled out of my lips. Though once they did, I knew they were true. Even if I'm not ready. But life happens in its own course, whether you're ready or not. I know this better than anyone.

"But I didn't," I reply simply.

Sebastian's anger deflates and he lays his head in my lap, face down, defeated. I stroke his hair, understanding how he feels.

After a moment, he sits up abruptly. "Why was Andrei even talking to Cliff in the first place? Why right then?" he asks suspiciously.

My brows bunch together as I get his meaning. "You think they were working together?" I ask skeptically. He raises an eyebrow, confirming his accusation. I scoff. "Cliff would never." I ponder it for a moment though before I realize what it must've been. "In my message to Andrei yesterday I told him I'd learned he never owned my contract. Cliff told me Andrei came looking for my last check. Andrei must've panicked when he knew the money would stop and tried to drain me for the last little bit before I could stop him. Little did he know, it was already too late. But obviously he got something else useful out of Cliff instead." I frown deeply, knowing I brought it on myself. I should've known better.

"Hey," Sebastian says, lifting my chin with a finger. "It's not your fault."

I gaze into his dark eyes, searching for answers. "How is it sometimes it seems like you can read my mind?" I ask.

He huffs out a breath and smiles. "I can't, Kira, I'm just paying attention."

His answer hits me in the gut. Because I'm pretty sure nobody has ever paid attention to me the way he has.

"Can we get out of here and go home?" I ask in response.

Sebastian smiles. "I'll find a nurse."

I lie back to rest, but Sebastian returns in what feels like moments. Or perhaps I fell asleep.

"I have news," he says, sitting next to me once more and smiling. So, it's happy news.

"Yes?"

"They're processing your discharge paperwork now," he says, borderline giddy.

I squint at him. "Okay …?"

"And the authorities plan to deport Andrei. They're putting through an expedited application due to the danger he poses. If all goes well, he'll be sent back to Russia and turned over to the authorities there in the next two weeks. Until then, he'll remain in police custody here, no visits, no calls, no hope for outside help."

I gasp. "You're *joking!*"

Sebastian grins. "Not even a little. You're free, Kira." The nurse opens the door and Sebastian laughs. "In every sense of the word."

14

SEBASTIAN

As Kira bursts happily back into the apartment, I have to laugh. I never imagined I'd see her so carefree and upbeat.

"Let's go see all the things, and eat all the food, and — oh! More chick flicks!" she demands.

I chuckle. "How about we see *some* of the things, eat all the food, and watch chick flicks?" I counter. "Remember, you still have a neck sprain."

She pouts a little before her face brightens mischievously. "True. Though you know what today is, don't you?"

I step forward into her space, slowly, in case she wants to stop me. When she doesn't, I swipe my hand down the side of her face with a grin. "The first day of the rest of our hopefully very long and very happy lives?" I murmur.

She blinks up at me in surprise. "That's not what I was going to say … but yes. I hope so too." She goes up on her toes and presses her mouth tenderly to mine. After a moment, she breaks away. "Today is also the day I can take this —" she taps her cervical collar "— off."

"Would you like me to do the honors?" I ask.

She steps back into my space this time, pressing up against me. "Yes. But … I want you to take it *all* off, Sebastian." She rubs against me, and I inhale sharply.

I place my hands gently on her shoulders, holding her in place.

"Are you sure, Kira? A lot has happened. I don't want to take advantage of —"

She pushes in and kisses me forcefully, her tongue tracing my mouth. And I may not have wanted to push her, but obviously Kira has a new zest for life. I fucking love it.

I lift her and she wraps her legs around me obligingly. I walk her into the bedroom, kicking the door open so I can set her gently down on the bed.

I run a hand down her cheek before undoing the collar and putting it on the nightstand. My fingers trace over her slender neck, brushing her hair back. I lean in, kissing her mouth, her ear, and all around her neck, as I press her back until she's lying down.

I slowly undress her, appreciating every curve and dip of her strong, petite body. Her gorgeous handful tits with dark nipples peaked invitingly in the cool air-conditioned room.

Her round hips, between which lay brunette curls fragrant with her arousal. Lean, strong legs I plan to have wrapped around my head soon.

As I'm putting her last sock on the floor, she whimpers, eyeing me with a hunger that ignites a fire deep in my belly.

I whip off my shirt and crawl over the bed, needing to feel her beneath me. She kisses and licks at my ear and neck, exactly as I did hers a moment ago. My cock strains against my zipper, so I pull away.

"You're still recovering, *mi cielo*," I murmur against her ear. "We're going to take this very, very slowly."

I kiss my way down the column of her neck, down her chest, licking circles around each nipple. She shifts and moans sweetly under me as I continue to work my way down, down, down.

When my mouth nears her hips, her fragrance overwhelms me. I bury my nose between her legs and inhale. "*Oh, Dios mío*," I groan into the soft flesh of her inner thighs. "You smell amazing."

She opens her legs widely, her fingers parting her nether lips. "Taste me, Sebastian."

Holy. Hell. Obligingly, I blow a breath over her warm, wet center. "My heaven, I'm not just going to taste you. I'm going to feast on you," I promise her.

And I make good on my promise, licking and touching and fucking her with my tongue and my fingers until she's coming undone, screaming in Russian as her pussy convulses in my mouth. I remove the two fingers I had inside her, offering them to her sweet mouth.

She takes them, hungrily sucking her juices. I inhale sharply as my cock twitches in my pants. Like she knows, she tells me, “I want to suck your dick. Now.”

I laugh and shake my head. “I don’t think that will be good for your neck, darling. Another time. I can wait.”

She yanks my hand until she’s pulled me close enough to get to my mouth, then kisses me fiercely. “Then fuck me. Please. I need more of you.”

I hesitate, unsure how far we can go without hurting her. But the desire to be in her is overwhelming.

“Show me your cock, Sebastian. I need it. I need you,” she begs, as if sensing my hesitation and knowing dirty talk was a good way to give me a hard shove over the edge. Her sudden switch to aggressive and sexual has me reeling.

In fact, I’m so turned on I can’t even respond. I barely get my fly open before she’s pulling at me, before I’m burying myself in her. And where I’d intended to take her sweetly, slowly, gently, we’re fucking like animals. I realize quickly it’s in part because she’s using her powerful legs to pull me in deep. Partly because she feels like heaven — *mi cielo,* my heaven — and I need her. All of her. Her expressive eyes, her blunt words, her laugh, her soft skin, her tight, hungry pussy. All of it.

But right now, it’s her pussy I need most. Even buried in

it, I'm in a frenzy for more. I pump hard until I'm sweating and moaning, Kira's hips writhing as she moans with me.

She grabs her breasts, bucks her hips, and calls out my name as she comes on my cock. As she clamps down around me, my balls tighten, and stars explode in my eyes as I come with her.

There are orgasms, and then there are sex-with-Kira orgasms. Holy. Hell.

Exhausted on every level, I pull out and sink face down on the bed next to her, slinging my arm over her torso. She strokes my skin languidly as we both pant from the effort of fucking each other senseless.

Once my pulse has returned to normal, I climb off the bed and go to the bathroom to clean up, coming back with a warm rag to do the same for Kira. She moans appreciatively and I almost want to go down on her again. I chuckle to myself. It's official: Kira Luan turns me into a sex-depraved maniac, addicted to the taste of her skin, her lips, her pussy.

"What's so funny?" she asks, her voice filled with sleepy satisfaction.

I chuck the rag in the laundry bin behind the door and rejoin her on the bed, stretching my body next to hers and kissing her deeply. "When you moan, it makes me want to eat you for breakfast, lunch, and dinner," I explain teasingly.

She gives a fake, exaggerated moan which abruptly devolves into laughter, and then I'm laughing with her.

"Seriously, though, is your neck okay?" I ask after the laughter has died down.

She turns her head slightly so she can look me in the eye. "Yes. It's okay. More than okay."

I lean in and nuzzle my nose against hers, placing a light kiss on her lips. "Good, I'm glad to hear it. How about I make us lunch?"

"I'm not lunch?" she teases.

I bite into my bottom lip. "Don't distract me out of actually feeding you," I tease back. "Or we may never leave this room again."

Kira's eyes go soft, and she puts a hand on my cheek. "If I get to stay with you, I'm okay with that."

I close my eyes against the swell of emotion her words bring in me. And when I open them, I know I'm staring at my future.

"As long as you'll have me," I promise.

15

KIRA

Five weeks later…

"Goddamn, Kira, if you don't stop, I won't get to fuck your beautiful pussy," Sebastian groans.

I pop my mouth off his delicious, wet cock. "Well, that would be a travesty," I tease. I press him back and climb on top of him, sliding down on his length to pleased groans from us both. And then I start to ride him.

His hands grab my hips, and he slams up as I slam down, the friction driving me wild. I land and twist in a circle, his dick rubbing all my spots, making my insides tighten. And the tighter I am, the harder he fucks. So I swirl again, tightening and climbing. He slams harder, over and again, until we're both crying out, my nails digging into his chest, his teeth clamping down on my shoulder as we come and come and come.

We sink onto the bed in a pile of sated limbs and barely quelled lust, and a sad thought settles over me.

"Once I'm back in the show, we won't be able to do this nearly as often," I lament.

With a smile, he kisses my lips sweetly. "We'll figure it out," he promises. "Speaking of which …" He lifts his head to get a look at the clock. "We need to leave for your appointment soon."

I begrudgingly follow him out of bed, clean up, and get dressed.

As we head to the hospital, I am unworried about the results. I know my neck is fine. And now, finally, so is my life. I had no idea I could feel this free, this happy.

We check in and wait until a middle-aged nurse calls me back.

"See you soon," I tell Sebastian, squeezing his hand. He smiles at me, and I grin back.

The nurse gives me a motherly smile as I catch up and follow her through the labyrinthian halls. We end up in a room filled with intimidating looking machines and she gestures for me to sit in a chair against the wall.

She confirms my name and date of birth, then gestures to a large machine behind her. "We're going to be using the CT to take pictures of your neck today. But before we get started, do you have any allergies?"

“Not that I know of,” I reply with a shrug.

“All right. And is there any chance you could be pregnant?” she asks.

I open my mouth to say “no” until I realize … I haven’t had my period. Not since before my accident. “I … do not think so, but I haven’t had a period for two months,” I admit. “Though they’ve never been very regular.”

“Hm,” she murmurs, making a note. “Do you use birth control?”

I nod. “Yes. I have the injection. Though it has been a while since my last one.”

“Well, you did experience trauma, and the stress on your body could have affected your cycle. But why don’t we do a test just to make sure?”

Nerves bunch in my tummy. “Is that really necessary? Is there not another machine we can use instead?”

“Well, we can do an MRI, but the doctor specifically requested a CT, so unless you’re pregnant or allergic to iodine, I’d have to get permission. Let’s just check, shall we?” She opens the cupboard and pulls out a small, cylindrical plastic cup. “Restroom is just there —” she gestures to my left “— and there are instructions with the supplies on the shelf.” She offers the cup to me with a smile.

Hesitantly, I take it. I walk numbly to the bathroom. I mechanically get the sample and bring it back. I watch her dip a strip into it. Then I watch her face light up not long after.

"Well, looks like we'd better do an MRI after all," she replies, holding the strip up for me to see. As if it made any sense to me. "You're pregnant."

16

SEBASTIAN

Seven months later...

"Cheer up, Sebastian, it's Friday!" Ty slaps me on the back with an encouraging grin.

I level an unamused look back at him. "It's Sunday, bro."

He lifts a shoulder. "Yeah, but it's *our* Friday. The start of three whole days off. Wanna hit up a strip club after this?"

I don't even get a chance to respond before Owen returns with another round of beers. He slides the first to me. "Drink up. You look like you need it."

I roll my eyes but take the beer and down it. He's not wrong. It also lets me avoid answering Ty's inane question. But like a dog with a bone, he doesn't let it go.

"What do you say, Owen? Our friend here looks like he

could use a lap dance, am I right?" Ty pushes, wiggling his eyebrows.

Owen snorts a laugh. "I'm pretty sure if Sebastian wanted to get some action, he would. And probably not at a fucking strip club."

My mouth quirks up but I fight the smile. At least someone has my back. You'd think it'd be my partner and friend of a few years, but no, it's his police officer cousin who just moved here three months ago. Go figure.

"You're both about as fun as a wet blanket. Come on. We're three single, good-looking guys in Vegas. There's got to be some debauchery you're willing to go in for," Ty says.

Owen shakes his head. "Unlike you guys, I've got to work tomorrow. But I'd be down for some karaoke. I think it starts in like twenty minutes."

Ty slumps back in the booth. "I mean sure, but we do karaoke every week."

I smirk over at Owen. Because *we* don't so much do it as *Owen* does after a few beers. Ty and I call him the Crooning Copper behind his back. But never to his face. The dude may be cool but he's one tough bastard.

Owen shrugs. "You guys can do what you want. I like it here."

Ty gestures around Enclave, the bar we hit up every week, sometimes a couple of times if it's a rough one. "Yeah, I mean, this place is cool. But it's the same old same old. And it's too off-strip strip to draw in the bachelorette parties if you know what I mean." He gives us a suggestive grin. "All I'm saying is, it might be nice to change it up for once."

"You just listed all the things I love about this place," I tell him. "But hey, if it's that important to you, you and I can go get into some shit after this." I continue drinking my beer. I'm going to need to build up a good buzz to put up with what Ty has in mind.

"Seriously? Fucking awesome!" Ty exclaims. "I've been meaning to check out The Palace. I hear it's expensive, but worth it if you know what I mean." He gives me a wink and an elbow nudge.

I shake my head. "Whatever, man."

"Sweet. I'll take that as 'I'm finally ready to break my dry spell, Ty, master of the universe,'" Ty jokes.

Owen cocks an eyebrow. "You really think you can get a stripper to go home with you?" he asks his cousin with a disbelieving look.

Ty points between our uniforms that we didn't bother changing out of due to our shift running over. "Wearing these? Um, yeah."

"Are you even allowed to do that?" Owen asks with a frown.

"Oh please, like you don't ever wear your uniform to impress women," Ty scoffs.

A cocky grin spreads over Owen's face. "I don't *need* the uniform to impress women, douchebag."

And that gets an actual laugh out of me. Ty's attention turns back to me.

"Aww, he's laughing. I think he's finally coming out of it. 'Bout damn time."

I don't respond, taking another drink instead. Am I coming out of the shitty mood I've been in for months? Maybe. More importantly, I realize that I'd like to. It's been exhausting.

So, I decide that I'll do my best to let loose with Ty tonight because it's been too long. I've been pissed off for too long. And even though I've long since stopped talking about it with Ty, he clearly knows my head's still not on right.

But how could I not be fucked up by what happened? That Kira just up and disappeared one day with no explanation or warning was just the beginning. Once I'd accepted that no amount of searching for her would help, my anger turned inward.

I'd been so eager to help her, to be with her that I'd set myself up for heartbreak. I practically asked her to use me and run. I was the idiot who got involved knowing she was going through way too much for her to ever stick around. And it's left me feeling like I can't trust myself, much less women.

But maybe it's time to start taking steps back toward life before Kira.

Fuck that. That's never going to happen.

It's time to start taking steps toward life after Kira. Accepting my utter failure is the first step. Lots of beer is the second. And maybe Ty is right, and strippers are the third. Kind of doubt it, but I guess anything's worth a shot at this point. Because God knows I can't keep living the half-life I have been since she left.

17

KIRA

"She'll never replace you."

I look over to find Michael at my side, his eyes on Coralie as she practices a complex series of moves that she's been struggling to make look as effortless as they should in front of an audience.

"She's getting better," I respond, resting a hand on top of my rounded belly. "And good thing, because I don't think I have much longer to train her."

Michael looks at me with a fond smile. "You could train her for years; she still wouldn't have your talent, grace, or stage presence."

I narrow my eyes at him. "What is it you need, Michael?"

He tips his head back and laughs. "From you? Not a thing, Kira, my dear." He rests a hand on my shoulder. "But I think you need to know that you'll always have a place here."

I scoff a laugh. "Yes, because Cliff doesn't want me to sue the production company for his slipup."

He lifts a shoulder. "That too, I suppose. I just don't want you to carry more stress. I think you've had quite enough to last a lifetime." He kisses me on the forehead. "I'm going to go clean up. Can I take you to dinner when you're done?"

I smile faintly in his direction, noting the hope in his voice. Always the hope, despite his knowing that my sole focus is having this baby. My mind can't think past such a huge change right now, and I certainly can't fathom Michael going from friend to anything else. Not as I'm about to become a mother. Not after all I've been through. Not when I'm not even sure my heart doesn't still belong to someone else.

"Thank you, but I'm going back to the apartment to rest," I reply, rubbing my baby bump for emphasis.

And just as every other time, I see the disappointment in his eyes, but as usual he hides it with a smile as he heads back to the dressing rooms.

Coralie finishes her sequence and alights on the stage with a grin. "Well?" she asks hopefully.

I smile wide and move toward her. "That was beautiful, Coralie. You're getting —" A sharp bolt of pain shoots through my middle and I double over.

I hear Coralie rush toward me, one of her arms wrapping

around my back as her other hand grasps my own. "Kira! Are you okay?"

I breathe through the pain for a moment until I'm able to speak. And then I nod, straightening up. "I'm okay. I'm not due for a couple weeks yet, but they warned me there might be false contractions."

Coralie looks skeptical. "Are you sure? I could go get Michael."

I shake my head and release her hand. "No, no. He's headed out. Don't trouble him. Let's just finish up here and —" Another pain cuts off my words, stronger and more spread out than the first. This time Coralie has to catch me before it brings me to my knees. It lasts longer as well, and deep in my bones, I know my time is up. "On second thought, maybe I need to get to the hospital."

Coralie calls out for Cliff, who appears from backstage, frowning. But his frown turns to concern when he sees me crouched with Coralie supporting me. And he freaks out.

"Oh my god! Is it time? It's time, isn't it?!" He starts hopping around.

I sigh heavily. "Yes, I think so. I —"

"I'll call an ambulance," he assures me, pulling out his cellphone and running back from where he came before I can protest, presumably to get Michael.

I close my eyes and breathe as another contraction hits. Hoping that the ambulance that comes for me is just an ambulance. And not a reminder of everything I left behind.

18

SEBASTIAN

"Four frequent flyers in one shift. Is it a full moon or something?" Ty asks with a tired sigh.

I clap him on the shoulder as we head back through A&E toward the ambulance entrance.

"Just one of those days. Good thing that's a wrap. Let's get this baby off the road and cleaned up." I look up as we approach our rig only to see another ambulance parked behind us and unloading.

I recognize the lead medic, Grant Tucker, who makes eye contact as his partner lowers the back end of the stretcher onto the ground. An obviously pregnant woman's cries echo through the emergency entrance area.

"Matern-a-taxi. They've got it," Ty murmurs, his eyes following them toward the hospital.

I turn to respond but get cut off by the woman's cries escalating, followed by what must be a string of curse words. But they're screamed in Russian. By what sounds like a voice I haven't heard in months. It can't be. Not *just* when I'd decided to move on. If it is, the universe sure has a sick sense of humor.

I turn back just in time to see them clear the doors, the dark-haired patient on the stretcher disappearing with it.

"Was that —" Ty starts.

"I don't know," I interrupt. I hover on the stretch of sidewalk between the sliding doors and the curb. It couldn't be Kira … could it?

Ty steps up beside me and I can feel the concern radiating off him. "Let's just go wrap up shift, okay? Then you can come back."

I chew on my lip, the urge to go find out *now* if that patient was the woman who tore my heart out and stomped all over it warring with my determination to put it all behind me.

"Dude. You *just* got off probation for running in ahead of the cops to save the girl. Don't do anything rash for another girl … or the same girl. Whatever. We'll go back, do what we're supposed to. If it's her— well, she's not going anywhere. Not for a while. Think, man."

I take a deep breath. He's right. And getting out of here will give me time to clear my head and decide if I even want to come back.

"You're right. It's probably not even really her. And even if it is I just …" I shake my head, not even sure what to say.

This time Ty claps me on the shoulder. "I get it. Let's just do what we have to do. Then you can decide what you want to do."

"Yeah. I guess that's as good a plan as any."

Normally I'm a pretty decisive guy. But when the woman you fell in love with disappears, leaving the key you gave her to your apartment, no note, and is untraceable after a series of terrifying events? It fucks you up a little. And in the end, my need for some sort of closure overrides my good sense.

Because Ty and I prep the rig for its next shift faster than I've ever done before and I'm back at the hospital, still in uniform, within the hour.

And I'm standing at the A&E desk getting ready to ambush a woman in labor just so I can move on with my life. Even knowing it's a jerk move, I can't stop myself. Marci, the evening intake coordinator, smiles up at me, seemingly oblivious to my inner debate, thankfully.

"Hey, Sebastian, thought you were done for the day?"

I tap the counter and smile nervously. "Yeah … I am. But when I was leaving earlier, Grant was bringing in a woman in labor …"

The surprise shows on Marci's face. "Uh, yeah, he did. She wasn't quite far enough along to deliver yet, so they went ahead and transferred her to the birthing center. Did you help bring her in?" She looks confused.

"No, I just thought it was someone I knew," I admit. Knowing I can't straight up ask for a patient's name that wasn't mine.

"Ah. Well, that's in their hands now. You can go up and check with them," Marci replies with an unconcerned shrug.

I take a deep breath and rap my knuckles on the counter. "I'll do that. Thanks, Marce."

"Sure thing," she replies with a smile, turning back to her paperwork.

The ride up to the third floor is a special kind of torture. I'm sweating by the time I walk down the long hall to the birthing and maternity unit. Not having a need to come here often, I don't know the nurse at the desk. She gives me a stern look as I approach.

"Hi, you had a patient transferred about an hour ago? A Russian woman?" I offer.

"Are you family?" she asks.

"No, I'm —"

"The paramedic." The voice comes from behind me. I turn to see a short, slender man who has just emerged from the hallway leading into the ward. He has cropped blond hair and is staring at me, wide-eyed. And he looks very familiar.

"Usually I just go by Sebastian," I reply amiably, turning

and offering my hand. "But you might know that, since I think we've already met."

He looks down at it for a moment and then back up at me but doesn't take it.

"Yes, we've met. How did you … what are you doing here?" He runs a hand through his hair and the gesture is hauntingly familiar.

And suddenly it clicks into place. That hand through that hair. The night I met her.

"You were in her show," I say. "You're here for Kira." Fuck. Kira is here. It *was* her.

His eyes dart guiltily around, confirming it.

I lumber forward and sink into one of the waiting room chairs, suddenly lightheaded. Kira is here. I realize on some level I didn't really think she was. Because on top of the fact that I may actually get some answers … that also means Kira is having a fucking baby. Some quick mental math doesn't make me feel much better.

I feel Michael sit down into the seat next to me.

I run my hands down my face. "Is she okay?"

"She's … great, actually," he replies quietly. "But I'm not sure if she'd want you to know she's here."

I bark out a sharp laugh. "Yeah, I caught that she didn't want me to know where she was, what with the disappearing and never speaking to me again." I sit up, leaning back in the chair and letting out a heavy breath. "The baby …" I don't even know how to ask.

"Andrei's," Michael says quickly, getting exactly where I was going.

I press my lips together and my nostrils flare. Even hearing that bastard's name sends anger shooting through me. "He's not … he was deported, right?"

Michael shifts uncomfortably. It takes him a while to respond. "I shouldn't be talking to you about this. You shouldn't even be here."

I shake my head. "I get that this is probably the worst timing ever, but I'm not going anywhere. I need to talk to her."

"She's in labor."

"Yeah, well, I hear that can take a while. Maybe she could use some company," I reply drily. And I'm sure as fuck not going to let her slip through my fingers again.

He rolls his eyes. "I was just going to pick up a few things for her. I wasn't going to leave her on her own for long."

My eyebrows bunch together yet, and I realize suddenly that Michael may be something to Kira I hadn't expected.

"Are you two together?" Even as I ask the question, I realize I don't want to know. That it doesn't matter.

Or does it?

Michael gives me a weird look. "Kira and me? We —"

He looks like he's about to say something else but stops himself. We stare at each other for a few moments. I don't know if that's confirmation or denial. Either way, clearly this dude isn't going to help me. Which makes me think at the very least there's something more than just friendship between them.

I rise and head back to the nurse. "Has the doctor restricted Ms. Luan's visitors?" I ask her.

She purses her lips. "No."

"And it is visiting hours, correct?"

Her eyes flick between Michael and me. Clearly, she heard every word.

"Yes. It is. But I'll need her permission to let you back."

My jaw tenses. Moment of truth. "Please tell her Sebastian Hernandez would like to see her."

The nurse hands me a clipboard. "Sign in. I'll go check with her."

She turns her back to me and heads down the hall. I watch until she disappears into the fourth door on the right before recording my name and the date and time on her sheet. And then I turn and meet Michael's gaze. I can feel his unease. And I wonder if he can feel mine.

The tense silence builds until I hear a door open and close and footsteps heading toward us. My eyes turn to meet the nurse's.

"Follow me."

19

KIRA

This is not how I saw any of this going. I thought I'd have more time to prepare. Silly me.

A harsh laugh escapes me as I pace the small room, my hands running unconsciously over my swollen belly.

Why should things start being predictable now? Nothing in my life has been. And I knew when I saw Sebastian as they brought me in that my time was up in more ways than one. On some level, I think I knew he'd find me eventually. Part of me hoped he would, even as I purposed to focus on becoming a mother.

Which was necessary. For me. For my baby. For our future. A future, I know, that will likely be as unpredictable as everything that has come before it.

I light knock on the door snaps me out of my thoughts. I

don't have time to respond before the door swings open and he's there.

Our gazes meet and my body stills. In his eyes I see the same warmth as always, now wrapped in deep sadness. He's still so handsome. And all at once, I feel all the emotions I've tried to stop myself from remembering. It's overwhelming. Damn pregnancy hormones.

"Kira," he breathes.

One word. Only one word, and it almost undoes me. But I must be stronger than that. I am stronger than that.

"Sebastian," I offer back firmly.

A small frown tugs at his lips. He gestures to my hand which is still absent-mindedly stroking my middle. "This is unexpected."

I snort a laugh. "Yes, for me too. But here we are."

He steps forward, and for a moment I think he might reach for me. My eyes widen and I take a step back. He halts, clearly reading my body language and stepping back himself, holding up his hands.

"I'm sorry. I know this isn't the best time. But I saw them bringing you in and I had to see you."

I dip my chin in acknowledgment. Not admitting that I'd wanted him to come once I'd seen him too.

"You look … strong, Kira," he remarks, tilting his head and examining my face.

"I was always strong," I reply with a small smile. "But it was you who helped me remember that."

He considers that for a moment before looking down into his hands. "And then you used that strength to leave me."

I blow a sharp breath out of my nose. "No, I left because I was afraid."

His eyes lift and meet mine. "But clearly you stopped being afraid at some point …." He trails off, but the unspoken words hang in there. And still, I did not seek him out. I knew it would hurt him.

"Yes. But it was because I realized I needed to learn to stand on my own. Can you understand that, Sebastian?" I ask, allowing some of the emotion I've tried not to feel into my voice.

He inhales slowly, then lets out the breath just as slowly before he responds. "I guess I can." He pauses. "Though I'm not going to pretend it didn't hurt. Did you at least get what you wanted?"

I look down at my stomach, smiling and rubbing it gently. "And so much more."

I settle down on the end of the hospital bed and gesture for Sebastian to sit in the chair next to it. He deserves an explanation, at the very least. He watches me carefully as I gather my words.

"I was going to get rid of it," I say, gesturing to my bump. "But when I went to do so, they told me it was a girl. They asked if I wanted to listen to her heartbeat. And I realized … I did. And it was so *strong*. Even though her origins were … messy, and unexpected, right away I realized

I couldn't punish her for it. That I had to protect her like I was never protected. It's given me purpose."

Sebastian leans forward, resting his chin on his fist. "I can see that. You sound … sure. I wish I … God, I'm a lot of things right now, Kira, but … I'm glad you're okay."

A contraction hits me before I can even think to respond, and I double over in pain. In an instant, one of Sebastian's hands is in mine, the other rubbing circles into my back.

"Breathe," he encourages me as I clamp my hand down on his.

I breathe as I learned in the classes, nodding my thanks until the pain passes. When I sit back up, I can feel the tears in my eyes. And not just from the pain.

But he doesn't let go. He gives me one of those looks I'd forgotten he's so good at. Understanding and comforting and loving. But he couldn't possibly still love me because I see the edge of anger there too. It hurts, even though I expected it.

The thought twists at my heart in a way that breaks through my resolve. Making me wonder again if my feelings for him haven't gone. The thought terrifies me just as much as my impending motherhood.

"It's possible to be strong and scared," he says quietly. Again, doing another thing I'd forgotten — talking to me like he's reading my mind.

"Right now, I just want to get this thing out of me," I

grumble jokingly as I scoot backward onto the bed so I can lean into the pillows.

Sebastian sits back down on the chair, perching awkwardly on its edge, watching me.

"I, uh …" He stops and shakes his head. "I have things I want to say, but now's not the time."

I close my eyes briefly. Not sure I want to hear those things. And yet somehow not wanting him to go. I cut him off completely for a reason; because I knew the mere sight of him would weaken my resolve. And it has.

"No, now is not the time," I finally agree, opening my eyes and looking at his expectant face.

"Will there be?" he asks curtly.

A lump rises in my throat and I lick my lips to disguise my discomfort. "No. Yes. I don't know." I shake my head. "I'm sorry."

He smirks and rises. "I should probably go before your boyfriend gets back anyway. I think I kind of pissed him off."

I frown, not understanding at first, but then realize he must have run into Michael. Anxiety ripples through me wondering what Michael told him.

But he presses on before I have a mind to form any questions or words.

"If it's okay, I can come back around the same time after my shift tomorrow."

I blink dumbly at him. Too overwhelmed to process any

of this. Too emotional to shut the door on him again. So, I simply nod.

He stares at me for a long moment. He's close enough that my heightened sense of smell from the pregnancy hormones picks up his sweat and shampoo and that smell on his skin that's just him. The memory of it does things to me.

"You're in good hands. You'll be just fine," he assures me. "See you tomorrow, Kira."

"Bye," I manage weakly as he leaves the room without hesitation. Almost like he doesn't really intend to come back. Not that I'd blame him if he didn't.

20

SEBASTIAN

"I'm an asshole. I can't go."

Ty rolls his eyes. "You're not an asshole."

"I'm a total asshole."

He tips his head to the side. "Yeah, okay, you're a little bit of an asshole. But you told her you were going to show. If you back out now …"

"So, you're basically asking me if I'd rather be an asshole or a pussy?"

Ty snorts and I can't help smiling a little. I rise from the bench, resigned.

"Going with asshole, then?" Ty teases. I roll my eyes. "Good choice, bro. Better an asshole than a pussy-ass doormat."

"Someday, Ty," I murmur as I walk past him. "Someday.

You're going to fall stupid for some chick. And when you have to choose between being an asshole and a pussy —"

"You'll be there to rub it in my face?"

I don't answer that that's not what I meant at all. That what I was going to say was then he'll really know what it costs you to forever want to put someone else's needs before your own. Even when it hurts. That's the power you give someone when you love them. I simply walk out, ready for more pain.

When I open the door to her hospital room, the sight of her hits me even harder than it did yesterday. Because this time she beams up at me with a tiny, wiggly bundle in her arms. My brain had somehow skipped over the whole baby thing, focused as I was on just seeing her. I force a smile and walk in.

"Hey," I greet her lamely.

"You came," she replies, gesturing me forward.

My feet feel like lead weights as I force myself toward her.

I stop at her bedside and take in her glowing face and the little bundle in her arms that has a shock of dark hair and pink bow lips just like her mama's.

"Beautiful," I murmur.

"Thank you," Kira says, cooing down at the baby. "I named her Nadia. It means 'hope.'"

I smirk and sink into the chair next to her bed. "It's a good name. How are you doing?"

Kira turns her full gaze back to me, scrutinizing my face.

"I've never been better. But I think maybe we need to talk about whatever it is that brought you here yesterday."

I lean back in my chair with a sigh. "You sure?"

She nods. "I think I need to hear it. To know what my actions did to you. I deserve to, anyway."

"You deserve peace," I murmur, shaking my head. Even now still protecting her from the question I know I need to ask. "And hope."

"Please." Her plea is simple and quiet, but forceful. So, I lean forward.

"Did you ever care for me at all or were you just using me the whole time?" The words tumble out just as bitterly as they've felt rolling around in my mouth all day.

I don't look at her. I can't. I know it's a totally unfair conversation to expect her to have right now. But when I see her hand reaching into my space, I look up. Tears fill her dark eyes, and mine follow. I reach up automatically and take her hand.

"I cared for you very much. More than I even knew until I left. Because aside from being terrified and needing to make the decision on my own, I also didn't think it was fair to ask more of you than you'd already given."

I take a deep, shaky breath and hold back my response, letting her words sink in. Because I'd have gladly done whatever she needed, and we both know that. Even if it meant taking care of another man's baby.

I nod, and the motion sends a single tear skittering down my cheek. Her brows bunch together.

"Are you crying because you don't believe me?" she asks, concern lacing her tone.

"I don't know," I admit.

Her frown deepens. "You don't know if you believe me, or you don't know if that's why you're crying?"

A broken laugh escapes me. "I believe you." Simple words. True words.

"But?"

I look down and stroke my thumb over the back of her hand. "You could've given me the choice. I feel … I guess I just feel like maybe I put myself out there too much. Gave too much, too fast, you know?"

She squeezes my hand hard. "You saved me. In more ways than I can …" She trails off and looks away, blinking hard. "I knew you'd be upset. But know that if it hadn't been for everything you did for me, I may not be here today." She looks down at Nadia. "She may not have been here." She looks back up at me, her eyes pleading. "But I am sorry if I made you feel used or like you did something wrong. That couldn't be further from the truth. My truth, anyway. And I hope someday it is your truth. You are a good man, Sebastian."

I slip my hand out of hers and scrub my hands down my face as I process that. On the surface, I get it. But the hurt and self-doubt this has all caused goes much deeper than that.

"Thanks," I reply hesitantly. "I wish I could say that makes me feel better, but regardless I appreciate the honesty."

The baby fusses in her arms and she bounces her gently. "Can I give you some more?" she asks, still focused on Nadia. I'm confused until she looks up at me and adds, "Honesty, that is."

Nerves twist in my gut. "Uhhh … I guess?" I reply hesitantly.

"I missed you," she says simply. "And I'm glad you're here. I know it's unfair, but I hope that we can be … I don't know, friends maybe?"

I lean back, stunned. That was the *last* thing I expected her to say. "*Thanks for dropping by, have a nice life,*" maybe but not "*Let's at least be friends.*" That's like … one of the worst ex slaps in the face.

I realize on some level that there's a reason that request is like twisting the knife. But I shove that reason deep down.

"I don't think that's a good idea," I say automatically.

And I'm a fucking doormat because the look of

disappointment on her face makes me want to take the words back instantly. But I stay strong.

"I understand," she says softly as Nadia's fussing ratchets up a notch. "I should feed her."

If her words didn't clue me in, Nadia's pawing at Kira's breast drives it home. And watching her breastfeed her baby is something I can't handle right now. I shoot out of my chair and back toward the door.

"Take care, Kira."

She looks like she wants to say something in return, but Nadia won't be denied any longer, and Kira is forced to turn her attention back to the baby. And it seems like as good a time as any to make my final escape before this woman tramples all over my heart any more than she already has.

"Ouch. 'Let's be friends' might be three of the worst words to hear coming out of the mouth of the woman you're in love with," Ty says shaking his head and taking a deep drink of his beer.

I snort and give him a look. "Yeah. Well. If I was still in love with her, sure. But it's whatever." I take a sip of my own drink. I *was* glad I found Ty already at Enclave when I got here, but now I'm not so sure.

"Seriously, dude?"

I look over at Ty to find him leveling me with a dead stare.

"Seriously, what, bro?" I ask, irritated.

"You totally still love her. At least don't lie to yourself."

My hackles immediately rise … followed by the equally alarming knowledge that they only are because he's not wrong.

"Yeah, that's what I thought," he says smugly.

I shake my head and take another drink. "So, what, you're all wise and shit all of a sudden?" I grumble.

Ty shrugs. "I just know you, dude. And I get that what went down sucked. But it only happened because you're the best dude I know, and you put yourself out there. Would you really rather that you hadn't?"

I set my glass down and give him an appraising look. "Jesus, you *are* all wise and shit all of a sudden." I pause. "No, I don't wish it hadn't happened."

"And you get why she reacted the way she did."

I shift uncomfortably. "Yes." The simple word sinks to the bottom of my heart. Because I do know. I know what she went through. Not that I can even begin to imagine how scared she must have been.

"Then give her a fucking break. Fuck, give *yourself* a break, Seb. Don't stop being you just because it bit you in that ass *once*."

I sit with that for a few minutes until both our glasses are empty. "You think I made a mistake? You think I should've agreed to be friends, even though I'd always be hoping for more?"

Ty grins. "Aaaand I just got you to basically admit you still love her and haven't totally given up hope. I knew my eternally optimistic brother-from-another-mother was still in there," he teases, clapping me on the back.

"That wasn't an answer," I point out.

He shrugs and flags down Shari, his favorite waitress. Equal odds to order another beer or ask her out for the thousandth time. Probably both.

"Dude, don't listen to me. I'm about to get shot down again. Clearly, I'm not someone who knows when to quit even when he should."

21

KIRA

I send Sebastian a text message from my new phone a week after I get home from the hospital, letting him know my number in case he changes his mind about being friends. Which I knew was selfish to even think, much less ask … but I had to.

The first few nights back were a blur, but we've settled into something of a routine already. And given the demands I usually face in a day, while I am loving the time with my daughter, my mind has too much time to wander.

It's strange thinking that this life was only possible because of Sebastian, and now he isn't even part of it. That was necessary for me to find my own footing, but now … well, I wasn't lying. I missed him. I *do* miss him. Even more … becoming a mother and experiencing pure, true love for my daughter has made me realize that I was close to feeling that for Sebastian. That I would've felt that for him if things had continued. That he's one of the only men I've met that I could trust with that kind of love.

That knowledge made it even harder to let him walk away, out of my life again. But he's not in my life because of my choices. And if he chooses to stay out, I'll have to live with that too. Which I fully expect him to.

That makes it even more surprising when he texts me back the next day.

I wish I could say I hadn't changed my mind.

My heart skips a beat in my chest. Does that mean what I think it means? I hesitate only a moment before replying.

So ... friends?

It's a good half hour before he responds back.

Maybe. But mostly ... I think I might regret it if I say no.

A grin breaks over my face. A few text messages back and forth later and we have plans for him to drop by Monday on his day off.

Three days later feels like weeks in baby world. Endless circles of feedings, changings, short bursts of sleep, and playing with Nadia have left me with no sense of time. Especially as Michael is at the theater rehearsing with Coralie most of the day nearly every day, not to speak of the multiple shows each week. So, I've pretty much gone it alone. In some senses, I prefer it that way. But knowing I'd see Sebastian again has woken feelings in me that have slumbered since we were together all those months ago. And I'm certain even when I suggested it, I didn't really want to be just his friend. But I could never ask him to take me back.

Even so, I've dressed in something other than an oversized nightshirt for the first time since I brought Nadia home; a simple T-shirt and jeans. And normally it wouldn't be a sexy look, but I *feel* sexy with my now milk-swollen breasts popping out of the top of the low vee neck that before Nadia showed absolutely nothing.

Still, when the doorbell rings, the nerves that have been making it hard to sit still all morning clench my stomach.

Opening the door makes them worse.

Sebastian greets me with a wary smile, looking more handsome than ever in fitted jeans and a T-shirt that shows off his well-developed arm muscles.

"Hello," I say quietly.

"Hey," he offers in return, then extends a bag toward me I hadn't realized he was carrying. "I come bearing gifts."

Tears prick the backs of my eyes at the thoughtfulness of the gesture, and I blink them away. Damn hormones.

"Thank you," I say, clumsily taking the bag and stepping back. "Please, come in."

He steps in, his wariness even more evident in his body language as his eyes swing around the apartment. And it suddenly clicks.

"Michael isn't here," I say as I close the door. And then add, "And Nadia is napping." I gesture toward the bedroom door just off the kitchen behind him.

He turns toward me, the corner of his lips quirked up. "Now who is reading whose mind?" he teases. But it sounds off.

I smile back, the odd tension between us stoking my nerves. "Can I get you something to drink?" I offer lamely, depositing the bag in an armchair as he takes a seat on the couch across from it.

"I'm good, thanks," he responds. "Why don't you open it." He tips his chin toward the bag.

I round the chair and take a seat, examining his face curiously. "But … why?"

He smirks and leans back. "Because when someone brings you presents, it's just polite to open them."

I roll my eyes. "No, I mean … why even bring them? Why come at all? I'm glad you're here, but … why?" I ask again with a shrug.

He takes a deep breath. "Because I realized I can't be mad at either of us for me being … well, me. And for you doing what you had to do."

I scrunch my face, still not sure exactly what he means when the word "presents" sinks in. I look at the bag, then back at him.

"Wait, *presents*?" I ask with a grin. "As in … more than one?"

He chuckles and gestures at the bag. "Open it, Kira."

I draw each item out, marveling at his thoughtfulness as I pull out a swaddle wrap and a pack of onesies, followed by two movies. I examine the covers.

"*Look Who's Talking* and *The Backup Plan*," Sebastian offers. "Both funny. Both have babies."

I purse my lips. I've heard of them. Both are also romantic comedies. But I don't comment on that fact, I simply catalog it and pull out the next item.

"York Peppermint Patties?" I ask, holding them up.

"My sister couldn't get enough of them after all three of hers," he explains.

"Ah." I reach down to retrieve the last item in the bag and let out a laugh of disbelief. I look up and meet his eye. "Nipple cream? You bought me nipple cream?" I grin at him teasingly.

He turns bright red. "Is that what that is?" He rubs the back of his neck self-consciously. "Yeah, my sister picked out the kid stuff, to be honest. She and I will have words about that one."

I laugh and collect the things, placing them all back in the bag.

"Well, thank you. And tell your sister thank you too, though I've already started switching to formula," I say.

"Oh? Why's that?"

I lift a shoulder. "Cliff has been very accommodating by letting me continue to work with my replacement and do other duties for the show. But with all the time I took off earlier this year, he was only able to give me a little over two weeks off for having the baby. And even that was difficult to get. So, I doubt I'll be able to continue to breastfeed once I'm back. Though that may not happen since first I have to find a place that will take Nadia that I can afford. I —" I'm cut off by the sounds of Nadia's shrill cries that tell me she's up from her nap. "Excuse me, I'll be right back."

I slip quickly through the kitchen and into my room — which is also Nadia's room as Michael's apartment only has two bedrooms. I lift her out of her crib and lay her on the bed to change her diaper, soothing her with my voice as I do. I bring her back into my arms and turn to go back only to see Sebastian leaning against the doorway. The unexpectedness and the expression on his face make my breath catch in my throat.

"You're a natural," he remarks, his voice deeper than usual. "It's a shame you won't get more time to be at home with her."

"Honestly? I love her more than I thought possible … but I'm not sorry to be going back to work. It means I'm that much closer to getting back on stage myself."

He steps forward and looks down at Nadia, brushing a strand of her dark hair from her tiny forehead. "She looks just like you."

I nod in agreement. "I'm thankful for that. She could've

looked like him. And I don't know what I would've done if she did."

Sebastian's hand falls back to his side. "And he's gone for good?"

I take in a deep, shaky breath and sit down on the bed. He settles next to me.

"After a fashion," I say quietly as I rock the baby. "He's dead."

Sebastian turns and looks at me in shock. "You're sure?"

I dip my chin. "I have a friend still, at the club where we met. She called me. She told me that when he returned, Andrei's father was waiting. He lost everything because of what Andrei did. Andrei knew he could never return, not because he was a criminal — really, he'd been one all along, so that was nothing new — but because of what his father would do to him for getting caught. And he wasn't wrong to fear it. It wasn't quick or pretty, from what she told me." I feel a tear slip over my cheek as I look up into Sebastian's dark, troubled eyes. "Am I wrong to be glad for it?"

He reaches up and runs his thumb over my cheek, wiping the tear away. "No. But … what about you? Does his father —"

I shake my head adamantly. "No. She said he'd assumed Andrei had killed me too before he'd left Russia. That he never even thought to ask after me. Though from the sound of it he didn't give Andrei much time to talk about anything." I shrug and sniff deeply.

"I'm so sorry, Kira," he murmurs.

My brows bunch together. "For what? I'm safe. I have a beautiful baby girl. A roof over my head. There's nothing for you to be sorry for."

"Speaking of the roof over your head … this is your room?" Sebastian asks, looking around at the obvious signs that both Nadia and I occupy the space.

I huff a laugh. "Yes. My room. Michael and I … it's not like that," I assure him.

He raises an eyebrow. "That's good to know." He shifts uncomfortably. "So, did you want to watch one of those movies or something? You know … as friends."

I chuckle and go to respond when Nadia starts to fuss and her head turns into my bosom, rooting for my nipple through my shirt. I rock and shush her. "Let me feed her here first, then I'd love to join you in the living room for a movie."

He nods and rises. And watching him go, I have hope that maybe we can be friends … and then maybe see where things go from there.

22

SEBASTIAN

"Maria, *please*. You owe me."

My youngest older sister puts her hands on her hips and gives me a look.

"You're so not over this woman."

"It's not about that. I just want to help her, and you know how hard it is to find a good daycare. And you're the best," I reply, buttering her up more than a little bit.

She rolls her eyes but smiles. "Yeah, yeah, yeah, *hermanito*. Fine. But I don't owe you for the truck repair."

"But that's two thousand dollars!" I say in shock.

She tilts her head and cocks an eyebrow. "I'll give her *three* months for that, Sebastian. That's a steep discount. But I want to meet her and the baby first." She pauses and narrows her eyes at me. "You're thinking about trying to get her back, aren't you."

I let out a deep sigh. "Honestly? I'm not ruling it out, but I'm still trying to wrap my head around all of this."

Maria pats me on the chest. "And yet you're still doing the hero thing, as always. Don't stop following your heart, *hermanito*."

I grimace. "Easy for you to say. But it didn't work out so well for me last time."

Maria smirks at me as she pulls a toy mallet out of a toddler's hand as he runs by. "One of these times it will. But only if you keep trying."

Once I get home, I text Kira to make plans for tomorrow, even though I only left her a few hours ago. I don't know whether to be surprised or not when she agrees. Either way, I borrowed an infant car seat from Maria just in case Kira doesn't have one handy. Kira's on a timeline, and I want to help her with this. Fuck all if I know why; it's sure as hell not my problem. And yet, here I am.

"You … want me to meet your sister?" Kira asks with wide eyes.

I realize immediately what the proposition must have

sounded like to her. "She runs a daycare," I explain quickly. "And since you need one for Nadia like …"

"Next week," Kira supplies quietly, then sighs, rubbing the hand that's not holding Nadia over her face. "But even home daycares are asking more than I can afford right now, Sebastian."

"Well, first maybe just check it out. And then we'll worry about how you'll manage until you're back on your feet, financially speaking anyway," I offer.

She cocks an eyebrow at me and quirks a smile. "We?"

I blush and rub my hand over the back of my neck. "I mean if you want my help. If not, that's cool too. I don't know. You needed a daycare. My sister runs one. Sue me for trying to hook you two up."

Kira full-on smiles and it knocks the breath out of me. "Okay, but I'm not sure how we'll get there. The car seat is in Michael's car, and he's at work. I wasn't expecting that we'd go anywhere."

I smile back. "That the best excuse you got?" I tease. "Maria lent me a car seat just in case. Go pack what you need."

Kira gives me a stunned look, seemingly frozen in place. And just as swiftly, she leans over and kisses me on the cheek. "Thank you," she says simply, then pulls back, blinking hard as she disappears into her room.

And now I sit on her couch, seemingly frozen in place by

the feeling of her lips on my cheek. The smell of her invading my senses. *Dios mío,* I am so screwed.

By the end of the day, Kira has agreed to leave Nadia with Maria starting next week. Thank fuck she didn't even question my sister's "free trial period" offer. Now I feel like I owe her for covering the fact that I'm effectively paying for it. I don't need Kira to feel any pressure from that gesture.

But seeing how happy she was watching Maria with Nadia, knowing her baby would be in the best hands possible … well, it's worth it. And the happiness her happiness made me feel cemented that I'm fully back to exactly where I was before all the anger. Totally head over heels for this woman.

I'm not even mad about it. It is what it is. Am I going to try to get her back? Hell, yes. Which is why, after dropping Kira and the baby back at their apartment, I wait for Kira to settle Nadia in for a nap before making my move.

I watch Kira slip quietly out of the bedroom, pulling the door to the frame behind her before joining me on the couch. She sinks back, leaning her head on the cushions and letting out a deep sigh.

"Thank you so much, Sebastian, you have no idea how relieved I am to have found such an amazing place for her," she says, lolling her head toward me.

I lean my head on my hand, examining her face. "You're welcome. But you look more tired than relieved," I tease.

She shrugs lightly. "She actually sleeps pretty well," Kira replies, gesturing toward the bedroom. "I guess I'm just … I don't know how to explain it. Being a mother is more exhausting than I imagined it would be."

I contemplate that for a moment. "Then maybe you need some time *not* being a mom," I reply. She gives me an inquisitive look. "When was the last time you got out of the house on your own? Did something just for you?"

Kira laughs. "Are you serious? I just had a baby, and before that, I was pregnant and generally freaking out. So probably since …" She trails off and her eyes go wide.

"Since you left me?" I offer. She nods contritely. I smile and reach for her hand, stroking my thumb over the back of it. "Then maybe it's about damn time I got you out of this house."

"Like … a date?" she asks tentatively.

The corner of my lips quirks up. "Something like that," I agree. "Or it could just be two friends going out and having a good time if you'd prefer." I pause for a moment, but she doesn't respond, so I keep going. "If you were to get out, what would you want to do?"

She chews at her bottom lip for a moment. "It's silly."

My eyebrows fly up. "Then you definitely have to tell me."

She scrunches her nose. "I'd just want to do whatever normal twenty-six-year-olds do in Las Vegas."

"So, drink, dance, gamble, stay out until the wee hours of the night? That sort of thing?"

Kira makes a disgusted face. "Not gambling no. But the rest … yes, that sounds … perfect."

I can't help but laugh. "You don't like gambling?" She shakes her head, the disgusted face reappearing. "Well, damn, you sure picked an interesting place to live, then."

The expression drops from her face. "I didn't pick it."

The smile likewise drops from mine. "I'm sorry, I didn't —"

She shakes her head. "It's okay. Yes, I would love to have drinks and go dancing and stay out late with you."

Nerves tighten in my stomach given that she didn't say whether it was a date or as friends. But she said yes, so I'm not going to push it.

"Really?"

She smiles shyly. "Really."

"Well, all right then. How does Thursday night work for you?"

Kira's eyes roam over my face as I wait for her to respond. And the nerves, the tension, the anticipation … it seems silly considering how many times I've had my cock buried in this woman. But so much has changed, and somehow this feels like it might be the start of something entirely new.

23

KIRA

I manage to get Michael to agree to mind Nadia Thursday night which shouldn't call for much more than one or two middle-of-the-night bottle feeds and changes that I might make it home for anyway. Well, depending on how the night goes. I purposely didn't say that it was a date not because I didn't want it to be, but mostly because I just want to see how it goes. I already feel like I'm taking advantage of Sebastian again, and guilt is a strong emotion. The feelings I have for him … well, they're strong too. It's just a lot, and I find myself more hesitant than I thought I'd be at his invitation.

Either way, it's almost seven o'clock and Sebastian is supposed to pick me up any minute now. I emerge from the bedroom after putting Nadia to sleep and changing into a strapless, sparkly little black dress and sky-high black satin heeled sandals I borrowed from Coralie.

When I walk into the main area, Michael gets one look at me from where he sits on the couch and his eyes nearly pop out of his head.

"You look … wow, Kira," he says, rising.

I blush self-consciously. "Thanks." I thought Michael's interest in me had passed, but the way he's looking at me suggests otherwise.

"Is that Coralie's?" he asks after a moment.

"Yes, how did you know?" I return suspiciously. It's not exactly something she wears to work.

He smiles mysteriously and settles back onto the couch but is saved from responding by a knock on the door.

I fix him with a look for a moment before sweeping past him to grab my clutch and answer the door, filing away that Michael may have moved on more than I imagined.

When I open the door, it's to Sebastian looking insanely hot in a black suit and tie with a light grey button-front shirt and black sunglasses that he promptly tilts down so he can exaggeratedly scan me from head to toe.

"Damn, Kira," he says, cocking an eyebrow and sliding his sunglasses back into place. "You look fantastic." Blinding rays from the late evening sun escape over his shoulder as he shifts, and I suddenly understand the need for sunglasses.

I shift too so he's once again blocking the sun. "You look

pretty good yourself," I reply, stepping out and pulling the door closed behind me. "Are you ready to tell me where we're going yet?"

"Dinner," he says with a charming smile, offering an arm.

I loop mine through his with a roll of my eyes. "I figured as much. But *where*?" I ask impatiently.

"You'll see."

I stick my tongue out at him defiantly for his non-informative response and he laughs.

"Just trust me, Kira."

I sigh and lean into him a little, not voicing that I do trust him because that means too much.

He drives us to the Strip, parking at the Bellagio and heading toward …

"*Spago?!*" I exclaim. "No! You're seriously taking me to Spago?"

He grins. "I seriously am."

"That's too much Sebastian," I protest.

"It's really not. Not for you," he replies with a small smile as he holds the door open for me. "Besides, I saved the sous chef's life a couple of months back, so he owes me one." He gives me a wink.

I shake my head and laugh as we head into the restaurant for what will almost certainly be one of the best meals I've eaten.

"Oh my god, that was the best dinner of my life," I moan as we exit the restaurant. I don't mention that it's also been the best date of my life. So much more relaxed than I'd anticipated, we simply enjoyed the food together and caught each other up on our lives. It was perfect.

Sebastian grins. "Honestly? Mine too. I'm glad you enjoyed it." He squeezes the arm I've got looped through his. "And I hope you're not too full because we're walking to our next destination."

"Lead the way," I tease, my excitement building at how he plans to top that dinner.

He takes us back to the car where he removes his suit jacket and tie, unbuttons his top two buttons, and rolls his shirtsleeves up to expose his forearms. Watching him do so is incredibly sexy. He also tucks my clutch into the trunk, and I hold my phone and a credit card in a small, invisible zippered pocket in my dress.

We walk down the strip for a bit, enjoying the flashing neon lights on the now fully dark, and fully packed, Las Vegas Boulevard. It's one of the few times I've joined in the nightlife on the Strip, and none of the other times were fun for me. But this? Walking with Sebastian and pointing out all the sights and oddities? Even this is far more fun than I'd imagined having tonight.

So, when we stop at a high-end-looking dance club

called Magenta, I'd almost forgotten that was our plan. And the idea of dancing with Sebastian sends a flurry of nervous, excited energy pouring through me.

He looks down at me as he holds the door open, his deep brown eyes glittering in the dark. I look up at him from under my eyelashes and smile.

When we get inside the club, we're shown to a booth and a waitress takes our drink orders. Sebastian slings an arm over the back of the booth, leaning toward me so I'll hear him over the thumping music of the dancefloor on the other side of the large space.

"What do you think?" he asks, sweeping a hand around widely.

I take in the lush fabrics of the booths, the clean crystal bar, and the not too overpacked dancefloor with well-dressed revelers and I lean toward him. "It's fantastic. I can't wait to dance," I admit.

The waitress returns with our drinks. Even the glassware looks expensive, and the garnishes are fancy swirls and shapes placed delicately in top-shelf-alcohol-based drinks. One sip confirms the luxury feel of the whole place. The drink goes down perhaps too easily, and we people watch together until we've finished our first round, then our second.

Finally, Sebastian slides out of the booth and offers a hand. "Ready to dance?" he asks with a tilt of an eyebrow. As I take his hand and stand, I feel a little lightheaded. His brows scrunch together. "Are you okay?"

I grin. "I'm *fantastic*," I breathe, tugging him toward the dancefloor.

He laughs and follows, and I waste no time burying myself in the crowd and twisting my hips to the music. I feel Sebastian slide up behind me, keeping his hands politely at my waist as he moves with me.

I groove and twist and let the music, the alcohol, and the utter freedom of being here flow through me. I toss my head back and imagine I'm performing, the hand motions and gyrations I'd normally perform mid-air coming as easily as breathing.

I feel Sebastian turn me and I open my eyes to meet his, dark and hard and filled with desire. He pulls me against him until our chests our flush, a first given the height of my heels, and I don't mind that it puts his mouth just inches about mine. Our hot breaths mingle as he leads his hips with mine, as the dance turns more primal. More heated.

It's not long before we're sweating in an increasingly packed crowd, but it doesn't shake his grip. Still, he doesn't touch me in any way that matches the heat in his gaze. And I realize I want him to.

I press away, overwhelmed by desire, not willing to give in to it for what it may mean to him. I snake my way through the crowd back to our table. I don't notice that Sebastian followed until he slides in beside me.

"Are you okay?" he asks, concern lacing his tone.

I nod meekly. "Just thirsty," I reply dismissively.

Sebastian gets the attention of a waitress and soon two tall glasses of water with lemon are placed before us. I sip mine slowly, relishing the cool liquid sliding down my throat, easing the knot that I hadn't realized had formed there.

"What happened out there?" Sebastian asks, not meeting my gaze.

I open my mouth to deny that it was anything but thirst, yet something in his tone makes me realize he knows that would be a lie.

"I'm afraid of you, Sebastian," I admit shakily.

His head snaps up, his gaze meeting mine.

"*You're* afraid of *me?*" he asks incredulously. And then he laughs. Like, bent over, holding his stomach laughs.

I let out a nervous giggle and he sits back up, wiping tears of laughter from his eyes. "I know, it's silly," I admit.

He shakes his head and huffs out one last laugh. "No, *mi cielo*," he murmurs, looking intently into my eyes. The use of those words transports me back to before. To being with him *that* way and my core tightens. "It's funny because *I'm* the one who's afraid of *you.*"

Guilt twists in my chest. "I'm sorry. I'm so, so sorry, Sebastian, you don't even know. If I could take it back, I would. I shouldn't have left. I should've told you everything. You cared about me, *took* care of me, in ways no one ever did, and I repaid you by running away, leaving you thinking you did something wrong. And still, now that you've given me another chance, I'm still taking advantage of you, and I feel like a complete asshole." Tears well in my eyes.

He scoots toward me, cupping my cheek in his palm. "It hurt. But I understand why you did. I just … forgot how broken you were because I was too busy thinking about how broken I was when you left."

I fold my hand over his and look up into his eyes earnestly. "Can you ever forgive me?"

Sebastian closes his eyes and blows out a breath. When he reopens them, they're shining. "I already have, Kira."

He leans in, his lips hovering over mine. But he doesn't move. And I realize he's asking for permission. I give it by pushing my mouth into his, and he lets go, his lips covering mine, his tongue pushing into my mouth, claiming and consuming me.

His hand strokes my cheek and neck as his tongue plunders my mouth, my own scraping along his in submission and want. When he finally pulls back, we're both breathless, forehead to forehead.

"Now that we've got that out of the way, I'm going to need to dance with you properly. Now." Sebastian's hard-edged tone belies his soft lips as they graze mine.

I nod, and he leads me back out for a dance that makes the one before look like nothing. With my back to his chest, his hands roam my sides, my thighs, and my stomach, as his hips guide mine in an erotic rhythm. His breath in my ear, his fingers grazing down my bare arms, his hardness against my backside … it all heightens the effect of the sultry beat and sweaty crowd.

I surrender to it. To him. To the night. Hoping the light of day doesn't betray the promise of tonight.

24

SEBASTIAN

As soon as I wake up on Friday, I knew I came on too strong with Kira. Went too fast. The woman just had a baby, for fuck's sake. And she's going back to work way too soon. Once again, she has too much on her plate.

In an attempt to slow my roll, I go over and hang out with her every night since Michael is working shows through the weekend. Just hang out. Nothing more. Thankfully the insane heat between us has cooled, and we spend time watching movies, eating take-out, and I even help a bit with getting Nadia to bed after dinner. Growing up in a Mexican American family, dealing with babies comes easily for me, though for some reason that surprises Kira.

Our whole dynamic becomes alarmingly domestic, and

perfectly chaste, as I head back to my own apartment every night after we finish whatever latest rom com we picked. I may be determined to take this slowly for her sake, but I'm just a man, and I'm not going to tempt myself like that until I know it's the right time.

But I don't have too much time to dwell on it, as I'm working an extended week of ten days on before I'll get four days off, and by the end of Kira's first week back at work, I'm exhausted. So, when Maria calls and asks me to stop by after my shift and after all her kids have gone home, I'm none too excited about it. But she insists.

"This better be good, *hermana*," I grumble as she lets me in. "I'm supposed to be picking up dinner and going over to Kira's."

Maria raises an eyebrow and clears some toys off the couch. "I'll just bet," she teases. "I'll make it quick, I promise." She goes to the kitchen and comes back with a box. "I'm going to hire some help for the daycare, but I want to drug test people who apply." She tosses the box at me. "The instructions are confusing, so as my favorite medical person, I thought you might be able to show me how to use it properly."

I roll my eyes and look down at the kit. "It's a simple oral swab," I respond. "It's not self-explanatory? And besides, couldn't you like, pay a company to do that for you?"

She rolls her eyes. "That's expensive, *hermanito*. This was like twenty bucks at Walmart."

"You just rub it on the inside of your cheek," I say, laughing at her. Maria always has been a little helpless with anything she deems "technical."

"Show me," she insists.

I roll my eyes and pop open the box, fishing out a swab. "Give me a bottle of water," I instruct. She hands me one. "First, you have them rinse out their mouth." I take a big drink, exaggeratedly swish it around, then swallow. "Then, you rub one side of the swab on one cheek for a minute, then you rub the other side of the swab on the other cheek for a minute." I open my mouth and demonstrate, letting her watch even though it's kind of weird. Then I hold out the slimy swab. "Then you stick it in the solution. It'll have a guide that tells you what you're dealing with based on what color the solution turns."

She snatches it from me and grins. "So, if I stick this in the solution, will it get you in trouble, *hermanito*?" she teases.

I scoff and stand up. "Is that it, Maria? Can I go now?"

"Almost," she stands up and grabs a plastic grocery bag from the shelf next to the window. "Give this to Kira. She forgot Nadia's empty bottles."

"So, I'm a teacher and a delivery boy. Great." I head toward the door.

"Thanks, little bro," she calls after me.

I wave my hand dismissively as I leave. “Stay out of trouble, *gordita*.”

I hear Maria laugh behind me as the door closes. And then I head to Kira’s. As I climb into the car, I realize I don’t miss going to my own place straight after work. Because going to Kira’s feels like going home.

25

KIRA

Life is good. I'm back at work, though under strict orders to take it easy for another week and a half. Nadia has been doing beautifully with Maria these last two weeks, and it's more of a joy than ever to see her at the end of the day. And Sebastian has been amazing, bringing food and taking care of us both. It was shocking seeing how well he changes diapers, feeds, and plays with Nadia. But that shock soon shifted to something else. And seeing him with her every night makes my heart ache in more ways than one.

As I collect Nadia on Friday afternoon, Maria seems antsy.

"Is everything okay?" I ask, concerned. "Did Nadia not do well today?" She's been having more trouble than usual settling for sleep at night, so I wouldn't be surprised if there was likewise some shift in her daily routine.

"No … it's not that. I just …" Maria chews on her lip.

My brows bunch together. "What?"

Maria scrunches up her nose. "I know it's not my place but … you never said who her father is and, well …"

I give her a small, pained smile. It's not the first time someone has asked, and I know it won't be the last. I shift Nadia to lean against my shoulder as I take a seat on the couch. Maria sits anxiously next to me as one last toddler that hasn't been picked up plays on the floor in front of us.

"I'm not sure what Sebastian has told you …" I start nervously.

Maria shakes her head. "Nothing. I didn't ask him. I figured if I was going to ask, I should ask you directly. If that's okay."

I nod and take a deep breath. "Sebastian helped me get out of a bad situation with Nadia's father. He was … not a nice man, and we were involved romantically for a while, but that ended before I was with Sebastian. Well … because I was with Sebastian, I suppose, though it had long been over for me," I ramble. Then I shake my head and collect myself. "Anyway, he was sent back to Russia. And that is where he remains. In a grave now, as it were." I grimace.

Maria purses her lips. "I'm sorry you had to go through that," she says. Except I can hear the "but" she's not saying.

"But?" I prompt.

She blanches. "How'd you know there was a but?"

I shrug. "Intuition."

Maria snorts.

"That's funny?" I ask, confused.

"Ironic," she admits drily, then hastily adds, "I'm sorry, that was rude."

I give her a confused look. "That's okay, but I'm afraid I don't understand what you're implying."

Maria rolls her lips into her mouth before she speaks again. "What if I told you that you were wrong?"

Now I'm really confused. Andrei isn't dead? How on earth would Maria know if she's only just learned of him?

"I'm sorry, I don't understand," I confess.

Maria's eyes flick down to Nadia, who is happily chewing her fist. "I had a suspicion. And the more I looked at her, the more I knew," Maria says, not really explaining anything.

"And?" I push.

"I did a cheek swab on both her and Sebastian," Maria says, drawing a paper out of her pocket, unfolding it, and offering it to me. "Sebastian is her father, Kira."

I blink hard. My heart drops. My head spins. I lean forward to catch my breath and Maria quickly takes Nadia from me.

I take a few deep breaths until I feel like I can sit up again and snatch the paper from where it settled on the couch between us. “That’s not possible … the timing …” I protest as my eyes scan the page.

But it isn’t just possible.

It’s true.

A simple chart lists numbers for “alleged father” and “child” with a very clear bottom line “Probability of Paternity.” And that number is 99.348%.

Sebastian is Nadia’s father.

“This can’t be,” I whisper. I look up at Maria, who is gently rocking Nadia. Nadia is beginning to fuss, possibly sensing my distress.

Maria gives me a sympathetic look. “I know this is a lot, and I’m sorry to drop this on you. But she has his eyebrows, Kira, how have neither of you ever noticed?”

I shake my head. “I guess you don’t notice what you don’t think is possible,” I murmur, looking down at the paper once more. Then I look back up at her, tears filling my eyes. “You’re her aunt. That’s why you gave me a ‘free trial,’ isn’t it?”

Maria shakes her head. “I only suspected late last week,” she says firmly. “You’re going to tell him, right?”

I take a deep, steady breath through my nose. My god. Telling Sebastian this …

“Of course,” I reply softly. “Though we just got back together. This is going to be … a lot. And if he stays with me, I’ll always wonder if it was just for the baby.”

Maria snorts again. “Not like he’s not already taking care of her even though he thinks she’s not his.”

My eyes snap up to meet hers. “What do you mean?”

Maria shrinks back, a clearly guilty look on her face. “Crap.”

“Maria?”

She scrunches her nose. “You aren’t getting a free trial. Sebastian paid for three months of care for Nadia.” My mouth drops open in shock. “But see,” she scrambles to explain, “he’s already all in, even though he thinks she’s not his. So, if he’s with you, it’s clearly because he wants to be.”

My head starts spinning. “I can’t … I’m not …” I lean forward, resting my head in my hands. I hear Maria rise and put Nadia in the bassinet next to the couch, then her footsteps head into the kitchen.

A moment later, a glass of water appears in front of me. I look up to see Maria offering it to me.

“Drink. And breathe.”

I take the water and drain the glass. And then I breathe while Maria rubs small circles over my back.

“Are you okay?” she asks after a few minutes.

I nod numbly. “I will be.”

“You’re not taking the bus home after this. I can drive you after Jaime gets picked up in about twenty minutes if you want.”

Tears well in my eyes as I look over at her. “Is your

whole family this nice then?" I tease, my voice thick with tears.

Maria laughs, wraps an arm around me, and gives me a gentle squeeze. "I guess we do tend to want to take care of people. Especially our own." She gives me a meaningful look that has tears spilling over my cheeks.

The idea of family, especially one that loves you enough to put your needs before their own, isn't something I'm used to. Though this news is overwhelming, maybe it will turn out to be a good thing. I hope.

But this is also huge, life-changing news. And I had months to come to terms with the fact that I was going to have a child. I feel like I am, once again, about to pull the rug out from under Sebastian, albeit in a very different way this time. I can only hope he doesn't run from the news the way I did.

26

SEBASTIAN

As soon as Kira opens the door, I know something is wrong. She doesn't say "hey" and give me her usual smile. Instead, she's radiating nervous energy and chewing on her lip like it's going out of style.

"Everything okay?" I ask as she steps back to let me in. I set the Chinese takeout I brought down on the coffee table and turn to find her twisting her fingers together. The apartment is completely silent and there's no sign of the baby. "Where's Nadia?"

"Maria took her for the night." She sits and perches on the edge of the couch. "We need to talk." She pats the cushion next to her, but I don't take the invitation.

"You're kind of freaking me out here, Kira," I reply.

"Please sit?" she implores me. And the anguish in her

tone is the only thing that could make me sit now that I've caught her nervous energy. But I also perch at the edge, facing her.

"Talk to me," I say. She twists her hands more fervently in her lap, so I take them in mine. "Whatever it is, I'm not going anywhere."

She huffs a sarcastic laugh. "We'll see about that."

Her anxiety suddenly makes sense. She has to tell me something. And she thinks I'm going to run like she did.

"I'm not going anywhere," I reiterate firmly. When she doesn't look at me, I grab her chin and turn her face, so her eyes meet mine. "Tell me what's going on."

"Why did you get back together with me?" she asks seemingly out of nowhere.

I swallow hard, not sure where this was going. "Because I still had feelings for you," I admit.

Her face tightens. "What kind of feelings, Sebastian? I need to hear it."

I close my eyes. This isn't like Kira at all. Do I admit it and risk scaring her off? Or do I hold back and risk not giving her whatever it is she needs right now?

I open my eyes, remembering when Maria said I had to keep trying.

"Because I love you, Kira. I loved you then, and I love you now. That's why I was so upset. If you didn't matter to me, I wouldn't have been so hurt."

Kira's face crumples. "I'm sorry I put you through

that. But you should know, I love you too. I didn't know that before because it wasn't until Nadia that I truly understood what that felt like. And I realized when you came back into my life that I felt that for you too. Everything you've done since then has only made me feel it more."

I want to smile, to laugh, to kiss her … but something about her countenance is still off.

"What brought this on?" I ask carefully.

Kira takes a deep breath and lets it out slowly. "Maria asked me about Nadia's father today."

I drop my hand from her chin and frown. Why on earth would Maria go poking around in Kira's past? That's a surefire way to stress her out, which is the last thing she needs right now. It could definitely explain why she's feeling like she needs reassurance right now.

Though I guess Maria wouldn't know that as I've never talked to her about it. But I'm sure as hell going to have a talk with her now.

"I'm so sorry, babe, that was out of line. I'll have a talk with Maria and —"

Kira puts her hand over my mouth, and I blanch in shock. "You don't understand. I didn't either. She saw something neither of us saw." Kira drops her hand and takes a deep breath. "Nadia isn't Andrei's, Sebastian."

My breath catches in my throat. Maria didn't know who Nadia's father was. The weird as fuck cheek swab immediately pops into my mind. Goddamn nosy Maria. But that means …

“She’s … mine?” I put together out loud. I look up at Kira. Her wary eyes all but confirm it.

“Yes. I had no idea. If I had, I wouldn’t have kept it from you. I hope you know that.”

I can hear the fear in her voice but it’s like a distant echo in my ears as my blood rushes loudly through my veins, making her sound far away. I start to feel lightheaded.

I’m a father.

I’m *Nadia’s* father.

I got Kira pregnant.

And she ran.

She did it all alone.

Hijo de puta.

I feel Kira’s hand on my shoulder, and I look up.

“Did you hear me?” she asks.

“What?” I respond dumbly.

“I asked if you need to lie down.”

I shake my head. “No. No, I’ll be okay.” I lean back against the couch, still processing. Kira sits quietly next to me.

“If you need to go, I’d understand,” she eventually says softly.

I look over at her and shake my head. “I’m just … holy shit, Kira.”

She nods. "I know. Maria had to drive me home, I was so upset."

Suddenly it's a like a lead weight has settled in my stomach. "You're upset that I'm her dad?" The words tumble out before I can stop them.

"No, no, no," she protests, grabbing my arm. "God, no, Sebastian. I'm upset that I didn't think it was possible. That I spent so much time upset because I thought I was carrying a monster's baby. If only I'd known, it could have saved so much hurt for us both. And I understand if you can't forgive me for that."

And for some reason, her asking my forgiveness again is what snaps me out of it. I lean forward and wrap my hands around her face. "This is not your fault," I say firmly. "All that matters is that we know now. And I'm not going anywhere." I put my mouth over hers before she can respond. Before she can voice her lingering doubts. Because those I'm going to erase for her right now.

I put every ounce of emotion I'm feeling right now into the kiss, letting my hands soothe her as they run over her soft, supple body. Over her enlarged breasts. Down under her ass, pulling her into my lap.

She sighs into my mouth and wraps her legs and arms around me. I lay her down on the couch, rubbing gently against her center as I move my mouth down to her ear.

"I love you, *mi cielo*." I kiss her on the neck. "We made

a beautiful baby, and if that's not proof of our love, I don't know what is."

She sighs contentedly. "I love you, Sebastian."

I trail kisses down her chest. "I need to taste you, Kira. Please." I look up into her liquid brown eyes and she nods, biting into her bottom lip seductively.

I lift her shirt and lick her skin, the saltiness of her and the scent of her perfume mix driving me senseless. I close my mouth over her bra-covered nipple, biting at her through the fabric. She arches into me, so I move to the other.

It's all too much and not enough. I bury my face in the soft skin of her stomach, smelling her arousal through her thin leggings. "I need you so fucking bad, Kira. Tell me I can be inside you."

She pushes at her leggings in answer, and I happily help her tug them off.

I need her too badly to wait. I unzip my pants, my stiff cock springing out.

"Shit, I don't have a condom," I curse.

She shakes her head, guiding me to her. "I don't care," she breathes. "Take me, Sebastian. I'm yours."

My cock jumps but my brain still has just enough blood left to hesitate. "You could get pregnant again," I say.

"And have more of your beautiful babies? I think that's one gamble I can live with."

I tip my head back, her words sending a bolt of love and

lust through my chest, straight to my aching cock, which I promptly bury in her.

Her wet warmth almost has me coming instantly, so I stay there, leaning in to claim her mouth until I can keep it together enough to claim the rest of her.

And then I move. Slowly. It should be too soon for this, but obviously, neither of us cares. I slide in and out of her as her hips follow the motion, her breasts pressing against me desperately as our tongues tangle and our hands wander.

Though I'm trying to be gentle, it's been so long. And not just for me, clearly, as Kira becomes frantic for friction. Soon we're going faster, breathing harder. Her slippery center is calling me back to heaven. My heaven.

"*Mi cielo*," I groan. Her mouth covers mine and I reach between us to stroke her into climax before I spill inside her. The small pressure has her clamping around me, milking my cock in seconds until we're both moaning into each other's mouth, my dick emptying into her. Her Russian curses meet my Spanish ones as we climax together.

Though we're both spent, I stay buried inside her. I rear up on my arms, looking down at her.

"I love you, Kira. And I'm not going anywhere. Ever again."

She squeezes me deeper in. "I love you, Sebastian. I'm not going anywhere ever again, either. I promise."

I sit up, pulling out and watching my come spill out of her. "No, you're not," I agree. "Because I'm going to spend all night owning this pussy. And then I want to see my daughter." My eyes flick up to hers. The love and desire and peace there hit me right in the chest. "Marry me."

She laughs and rears up, kissing me lightly. "You don't have to prove anything. And you don't have to marry me to make sure I don't leave."

I grasp her chin firmly. "And if I want to marry you because I love you? Because you're the mother of my child? Because I want a family with you? I want to be everything for you, Kira. I want to be there to raise Nadia and watch her grow into a beautiful, strong woman like her mother. And I want to make more beautiful babies with you when you're ready. So I'm seriously asking. Will you marry me, Kira?"

Her eyes are dark and intense as she looks at me in wonder. "Yes."

My mouth quirks up into a smile. "Yes?"

She grins. "Yes." Her eyes trail down my body. Her eyes on my cock make him stand to attention again. She bites into her lip and looks up at me. "Now claim what's yours." She lays back and spreads her legs in invitation, which only makes me harder for her.

I fist my cock and run it through her wet folds, teasing her clit with it. "Oh, I'm going to. Over." I slide in and she moans. "And over." I pump into her slowly and she writhes against me. "And over." I lean into her and kiss her deeply. "Forever."

She moans into my thrusts, her nails raking down my

back. “Yes, God, please, yes. Forever, Sebastian. Promise me forever again.”

And as I make love to her all night, I promise it to her over and over. Because we were meant for each other. Only fate could’ve brought us together like this. Only fate could have made Nadia my daughter. And as sweet as words whispered while I’m inside her are, I fully intend to make good on that promise every day for the rest of forever.

EPILOGUE

KIRA

Four years later…

"Daddy, Tia Isabel said I could have *two* pieces of cake!" Nadia exclaims happily to my husband.

Sebastian shakes his head and glares daggers across the backyard at his eldest sister, who just smirks back at him as all three of her kids dance circles around her. His gaze shifts to me in an unmistakable *"Can you believe her?"* look.

I shift Diego to my other shoulder and shrug, trying not to smile. Isabel is always trying to wind Sebastian up and I not-so-secretly find it hilarious.

One of the many pleasant surprises I received when I joined this family and married Sebastian three years ago.

"Do you want me to take him?" Maria asks, sidling up to me.

I throw her a grateful smile and heft the baby into her arms.

"Oof," she jokes. "I always forget how substantial he is for a ten-month-old."

"He's a whole lotta love," I reply, booping him on the nose. "I'm going to go talk Sebastian off the ledge."

Maria laughs. "Good luck with that. Isabel's been poking at him all day."

I smile and leave her to baby-duty which, despite her being so darn good at that it's been her career for years, she's yet to have any of her own. Sebastian's parents aren't happy about that, but she's happy being the awesome auntie she is, and I can't say I mind all the help she gives.

"Honey," I say softly, touching Sebastian on the shoulder.

He turns toward me, a smile breaking over his handsome face. Then it drops. "Where's Diego?" he asks.

I turn and point to Maria who waves at him, rolling her eyes. He's such a protective daddy.

Sebastian cocks an eyebrow at me. "You're baby free?"

I laugh. "And Nadia has gone to play with her cousins," I point out, raising an eyebrow back.

He wraps his arms around my waist and pulls me to him. "Mmmm," he murmurs, leaning in to kiss my neck. "Maybe we should sneak away and get some time just for us."

"Hey, keep it in your pants, *hermanito*," Isabel snaps as she walks by. "This is a kid's birthday party for fuck's sake."

I burst out laughing at her obvious hypocrisy as Sebastian starts yelling after her in Spanish. Which I've learned enough of by now to know it's nothing nicer than what she just said in English.

"Hey, the kids can understand Spanish too," I remind him.

He frowns and makes a rude gesture at Isabel, effectively ending the argument.

"Yeah, well, she started it," he says.

I tug on his hand, leading him toward the house. "Come on. I think some time just for us is exactly what you need."

His smile returns in force. "Can we have sex in my childhood bedroom?" he asks in a low voice.

I laugh as I pull him inside. "We're not having sex in your parents' house," I chide, shaking my head. But I wrap my arms around his neck and pull myself up for some child-free make-out time.

He sinks into me, happily going along with that plan.

After a few minutes, he pulls back. "I still can't believe you put up with my crazy family," he murmurs with a smile.

I smile back up at him. "I love your crazy family. *Our* crazy family."

"And I love you."

"Mmm," I hum. "And would you love me if I was already pregnant again?"

His eyebrows shoot up. "No!" he exclaims. "Really?"

I grin. "Really. But it's early, so shush."

Sebastian's hands wrap around my face, his eyes liquid with heat and love. "Are you okay? You've only been back performing again for a few months. I know how much it means to you."

"About that," I say. "I'm actually … surprisingly not as into it as I once was. I think after this little guy —" I rest my hand on my lower belly "— I might go into teaching."

"Really?" he asks thoughtfully. "That's something you'd be interested in full-time?"

I shrug. "Training someone new this last time … well, I forgot how rewarding it could be to watch someone learn and grow. And honestly, I'm enjoying making all these babies with you, husband of mine." I grin slyly and give him a small kiss.

"Oh, are you?" he responds, grinding his pelvis into me. His massive erection surprises me.

"Sebastian!" I exclaim in surprise.

He grins. "What? Hearing I got you knocked up again turns me on." He leans in and kisses the spot under my earlobe. "Come on. Let's go upstairs and celebrate." His hand trails down and works my nipple as his mouth suckles my neck. Heat pools between my thighs and I sigh against him.

"Am I always going to be this weak for you?" I reply with a moan.

"Is that a 'yes'?" he whispers against my ear, sending shivers down my spine.

"That's a yes," I confirm, knowing I'm going to need him inside of me to relieve the ache he just started.

"Then I hope you're always this weak for me. Because I am for you, *mi cielo.* And God willing, I always will be."

I grab him through his pants, and he sucks in a breath.

"Forever?" I ask.

He lifts me abruptly, carrying me up the stairs. "Forever," he promises.

A NOTE FROM THE AUTHOR

Thank you so much for reading! Now … I need your help! Will you please take a minute to leave a review? It doesn't have to be long — just a couple of sentences saying what you thought of the book on Amazon, goodreads, and/or BookBub. Your opinion is important to potential readers and to me. Thank you!

ABOUT THE HOT VEGAS NIGHTS SERIES

I hope you enjoyed my book, *Vegas Baby*, which is part of the shared world Hot Vegas Nights. Would you like to read all of them? Find them here on Kindle Unlimited.

The Vegas Strip is the gateway to your wildest fantasies. Where debauchery rules and depravity runs rampant. Elusive billionaires, celebrity bad boys, tantalizing dancers, master mixologists, and sexy tattoo artists are all within reach.

During these 17 Hot Vegas Nights, you'll take a chance on love, lose yourself in entertainment, and gamble your heart away! Seventeen books that are all written with your pleasure in mind.

Vegas Storm by D.M. Davis

Vegas Baby by Melanie A. Smith

Vegas Price by Mckenna James

Vegas Showdown by Amy Stephens

Healing in Vegas by Sydney Aaliyah Michelle

Vegas Reward by Michelle Donn

Playing Vegas by CL Collier

What Happens in Vegas by Sabrina Wagner

The Vegas Pitch by Amanda Shelley

Escaping Vegas by S.A. Clayton

Waking up Married in Vegas by Kaylee Monroe

A Vegas Dare by Kate Stacy

Vegas Valet by TL Mayhew

Vegas Redemption by Anise Storm

All's Fair in Love & Vegas by Shannon O'Connor & M Leigh Morhaime

Vegas Lights by Cala Griffin

Vegas Jackpot by E.M. Shue

ACKNOWLEDGMENTS

This year has been rough, but I'm so proud and happy to have finished this story. I couldn't have done it without the help of so many people.

First thanks always go to my family, my husband in particular for listening, encouraging, and lifting me up every day.

A huge thanks to my book bestie, Eve Kasey, not only for beta reading this story, but for being one of the most awesome cheerleaders, shoulders to cry on, and human beings I know.

And speaking of shoulders to cry on, a huge thanks to the phenomenal Harlow James for commiserating on everything authorly and beyond. There are so few people who I can talk candidly with and I value your friendship so much.

Thanks to Jenny Gardner, my OG bestie and partner in editing crime. Our friendship is now almost old enough to rent its own car. Miss you lots!

Tapadh leat to my favorite Scot, my sister of the Anne with an "e" clan. Your friendship was an unexpected gift of my author journey, and I’m so glad to have “met” you … and hopefully someday I’ll actually meet you!

And a huge thank you to YOU for reading this book. I truly hope you enjoyed it.

ABOUT THE AUTHOR

Melanie A. Smith is a former engineer turned stay-at-home mom and award-winning, international best-selling author of steamy contemporary romance. She crafts strong book boyfriends with hearts of gold and smart, self-sufficient heroines. When she's not lost in the world of books, you'll find her spending time with family, cooking, and driving with the windows down and the stereo cranked up loud.

facebook.com/MelanieASmithAuthor
twitter.com/MelASmithAuthor
instagram.com/melanieasmithauthor

BOOKS BY MELANIE A. SMITH

The Safeguarded Heart Series

The Safeguarded Heart

All of Me

Never Forget

Her Dirty Secret

Recipes from the Heart: A Companion to the Safeguarded Heart Series

The Safeguarded Heart Complete Series: All Five Books and Exclusive Bonus Material

Life Lessons: A series that can be read as standalones

Never Date a Doctor

Bad Boys Don't Make Good Boyfriends

You Can't Buy Love

The Heart of Rutherford: Life Lessons Novels 1 – 3

Standalone Romance Novels

Everybody Lies

Last Kiss Under the Mistletoe

Tough Love

Finding His Redemption

Short Stories

Lightning Source UK Ltd.
Milton Keynes UK
UKHW040639041122
411637UK00004B/326